I0654202

THE CONSPIRACY GAME

JUSTINIA WRIGHT PRIVATE INVESTIGATOR MYSTERIES
BOOK 4

C W HAWES

CWH BOOKS KATY, TEXAS

Paperback ISBN: 978-1-942376-42-2

Cover by Raihana Dewji

❀ Created with Vellum

This one is for my sister, with thanks.

JOIN THE TEAM!

I invite you to become a VIP Reader. You'll get a free copy of *Vampire House and other early cases of Justinia Wright, P.I.* right off the bat.

Then once a month, maybe more often, you'll get a variety of good things to keep you up to date with my many worlds, as well as curated content.

Just click, tap, or scan the QR code to begin the adventure!

1

SHE'S NOT HERE

Friday Night into Saturday Morning. September 19th to 20th

CUT A FLATWORM IN HALF AND YOU GET TWO FLATWORMS. Unfortunately, private investigation agencies aren't flatworms. Take the best detective out of the agency and you're left with an agency that doesn't have its best detective.

Which helps explain why Bea, my wife and assistant, was at home in the office holding down the fort, while Ed Hafner and I were sitting in my car waiting for a man by the name of Darren Clay to emerge from the bar we'd tracked him to. I was getting paid all of $475 to find the guy and serve him the summons. And because Ed was sitting next to me, I wouldn't get to keep all of it.

Ed is one of the three freelancers Tina hired when she needed extra hands, feet, ears, and eyes. Only Tina didn't hire him. I did. Harry Wright, the guy now running Wright Investigations.

"Any idea when she's coming back?" Ed took a bite out of his burger. The "she" he was referring to was Tina, my sister, and the Justinia Wright behind Wright Investigations.

"No. I don't even know where the hell she is, Ed."

"I don't mean to pry, but that must've been one helluva big fight she and Lieutenant Swenson had."

"It was big. In fact, it was gargantuan."

Tina and Cal Swenson have been on and off lovers since before I came to live and work with her, some half-dozen years ago. Through it all, they remained friends. However, this time was different.

Not only did Cal read her the riot act for withholding evidence and obstructing justice, he threatened to yank her license, and told her he was sleeping with his partner and wouldn't be coming back to live with her.

Couple the threat and the revelation with the fact Tina pulled a gun on him and, yeah, it was very much one helluva big fight.

Four days later, Tina packed a suitcase and left. Not one word as to where she was going or what she'd be doing. Nothing. Nada. Zip. Zilch. Just said, "goodbye", and that she'd be in touch.

And keep in touch she did, up until six weeks ago. A weekly text message saying she was fine and then, "I'll be out of touch for awhile. Always remember, I love you, Harry. Bea, too." And that was it. Now nothing and I'm worried sick about her.

Bea and I have done what we can to keep the home fires burning. We've fed her cats. We've kept the agency open taking whatever work comes our way. It's not a lot, though. Without Tina, Wright Investigations is just one among many.

The work, such as it is, does keep Bea and me in practice. We've also learned shorthand. Just in case. One can't always use a digital recorder and being able to take down a conversation in shorthand seemed to me to have its advantages.

Ed was shaking his big head. "Yeah, that's too bad. Me and the missus, we have us a doozy every now and then. But we always work it out. Got the kids, ya know?"

"Kids make a difference."

"They sure do. Makes ya think about something other than yourself."

Our quarry emerged from the bar. "Okay, Ed, here we go."

We got out of the car and made for the intended recipient of the summons I had in my hand. He was preoccupied with the hotty on his arm. Ed and I moved in. He got behind the couple and I positioned myself in front.

"Darren Clay?" I asked.

"Who wants to know?"

"I do. I have something for you, if you're Darren Clay."

"Get the hell outta my face."

He took a swing at me and I got out of the way just in time.

Ed grabbed him and the hotty started screaming. I turned to her and she took off running back to the bar. A crowd was beginning to gather. Ed had Clay in a half-nelson. I shoved the papers into Clay's jacket pocket, told him he was served, and headed for my car. Ed let him go and the clown ran up behind me, pushed me down, and smacked my left cheek with his fist when I started to get up. That was before Ed caught up and koshed him a good one. Clay dropped to the pavement like a sack of groceries.

A guy from the crowd charged Ed and got backhanded by Ed's sap. He too lay crumpled on the ground.

A siren was blaring and a cop car pulled into the bar's parking lot, screeching to a halt. The crowd vanished at the same time an amplified voice told everyone to freeze.

"Aw, hell," Ed muttered.

We froze and two officers got out, guns drawn. They got within ten feet of us when one of them said, "Harry Wright, is that you?"

I recognized the voice and face. "Hi, Josh. Yeah, it's me."

"What the hell's going on?" Josh motioned to his partner and they holstered their weapons.

"Just serving a summons to this fellow." I pointed to Clay. "He didn't want to be served. Took a swing at me, I served him, then he pushed me down and punched me. Ed, here, incapacitated him."

"And that guy?" Josh point to the other fellow, who was now picking himself up off the pavement.

"He attacked Ed and Ed defended himself."

"Ed work for you?" Josh asked.

"Yes."

Josh turned to his partner. "They're okay, Seth. I know Harry. Helped stop my daughter from being kidnapped four years ago."

Clay was getting up. "I want to press charges. They attacked me."

Josh turned to Clay. "Were you served a summons?"

"It's in his coat pocket," I volunteered.

"What's the summons for?" Josh asked.

"Domestic violence," I answered.

"Shit." Josh's tone of voice and the look on his face were not at all friendly. "Get the hell outta here before I beat the crap out of you myself."

Clay spat. "Cops. Mofo bastards."

"Get the hell outta here and get out fast." Josh's voice was quiet, but there was plenty of emotion in it and not the kind indicating he wanted to be best friends.

Clay and the other fellow left.

Josh turned to me. "Nothing to worry about, Harry. Go home and get some ice on that shiner."

"Thanks, Josh."

We shook hands.

Ed and I got into my Focus. I started it up, put it in drive, and began the trip to Ed's place to drop him off.

"So you rescued his daughter?" Ed asked.

"Stinky, actually. I was there, but Stinky's the one who talked the guy into letting her go."

"Yeah, that'll earn ya some points. Sure miss Stinky. Wasn't much to look at. Sure did get results, though."

"That he did. Our lucky night Josh answered the call."

"Yeah. Should buy a lottery ticket."

"Maybe two."

"Yeah. Maybe two."

The time was twelve after two when I walked through the back door. The lights were on, which meant Bea was waiting for me. Buddy, her Affenpinscher, greeted me, tail wagging. I scratched behind his ears and walked on into the living room, where I found my honey lying on the couch with Isis, Tina's Sphinx cat, cuddled next to her, both sound asleep. I leaned down and kissed her.

"Hi, Hon, I'm home. Let's go to bed."

Her eyes fluttered open. "Hi, Harry." She reached up to touch my face. "Oh, my God! Harry, you're hurt! Let me get ice." She got off the couch. "Lie down."

"Bea—"

"Lie down. I'm taking care of my man."

I couldn't help but smile. "Okay, Buttercup."

Into the kitchen she went and Isis was relegated to the floor where she was joined by Prudy, Tina's Maine Coon, Manly, Tina's Manx, and Buddy. The critters sat in a row looking at me to see what all the fuss was about. In a minute Bea came back with an ice bag and towel. She put the ice on my face and I held it there.

"Get the Arnica from the medicine cabinet, would you please? It'll take care of the bruising or at least lessen it."

"Okay." And off she went. Soon my little Bea was back with the medicine and a spoon. She sat next to me on the couch. At five-three and not even a hundred pounds, she doesn't take up much room. I put a couple tablets into my mouth and let them dissolve under my tongue.

"Speaking of 'Buttercup'," Bea said, "Cal stopped by earlier."

"He did? What did he want?"

"He wanted to see Tina. I told him she wasn't home and I didn't know when she'd be back. He seemed at a loss for words, so I invited him in. He then asked if she'd be available tomorrow.

"I said, 'I don't think so, Cal. She's not here.'

"He said, 'Look, Bea, I know you're—'

"And I said, 'Honest, Cal, she's not here. Hasn't been for months.'

"When I said that he mouthed the word 'months' and sat on

the deacon's bench. I said, 'Yeah. She's been gone for like six months, I think.'

"He was like in shock and just sat there for awhile. I sat next to him. I held his hand. I think he needed it."

"Probably."

"Then he asked if she was seeing someone and I told him I didn't know because we haven't heard from her in like six weeks. He turned his head and looked at me and said, 'Really?' And I said, 'Yeah.' He looked down at his hands and put the hand I wasn't holding over mine.

"He was quiet for quite awhile, finally he said, 'I've really messed this up. Nikki and I aren't seeing each other anymore. She's even gone back to Vice and uh, I... Aw, shit, Bea. I love Tina and I really screwed things up royal.'

"I said, 'You *were* pretty shitty to her, Cal, and hurt her really bad.'

"His voice was very soft. I almost didn't catch it. He said, 'I know.'

"Then he got kind of official and said, 'You haven't heard from her in six weeks? Have you notified anyone?'

"I said, 'Cal, who can we notify? We don't have any idea where she is.'

"He stood and said, 'I'll see what I can find out. I'll let you know.'

"We said goodbye to each other and he left."

"Interesting, hon. It might be a case of too little too late. Tina isn't going to forget what he did and to be honest I can't blame her."

"I know, Harry. That's what's so sad. I thought I messed up relationships. Those two... They take the cake. They're crazy in love with each other and constantly blow it up."

"Yes, they do. It's pretty bizarre if you ask me."

"It is. Let me see your face."

I took away the ice and she leaned down and kissed the bruise.

"That's to make the owie go away."

She moved to my lips and kissed them. I put my arms around her and kissed her back. The kiss deepened and when our lips parted, she murmured, "I love you, Harry."

I whispered back, "I love you, Beatrice."

She giggled. "That's a mouthful."

"It is."

"Here. Let me fill your mouth with something else." She kissed me, filling my mouth with her probing tongue. She started to withdraw and I sucked it in, held it, then let go.

She sat up and took off her shirt and I lightly ran my fingers across her bare flat chest. Her little nipples were erect and hard. I raised my head and kissed each one.

"Take me to bed, Harry." She stood.

I got off the couch, scooped her up in my arms, and climbed the stairs to our room, kissing her all the way. Then, in our bed, we loved each other for a long, long time.

———

Bea is the most passionate person I know. In our lovemaking it is no holds barred with her. And to think she was so insecure when I first met her. All she needed was someone to accept her and love her for who she is. When I did, she burst into bloom. She's become a confident woman and doesn't take much crap from anyone.

Before she came into my life, things were okay. Now? Without her, life would be a great big black hole.

Tina and Cal are the same really. They love each other and are good together. However, each one is afraid of something and, whatever it is, it tears apart two people who should be together and too often aren't.

2

LIQUID NIGHT

Early Sunday Morning. September 21st

THE ALARM WENT OFF AT SIX. EARLY FOR A SUNDAY MORNING, I know, but Bea and I were working on a case. We needed to be at Summer Tollefson's townhouse to photograph dew on Dale Arneson's car, as well as the "V" I'd marked with permanent marker on the rear passenger-side tire.

All this to prove Dale was violating his separation agreement with his soon to be ex-wife, Judith. She was of the opinion Dale's girlfriend, Summer, was a bad influence on little Jimmy Arneson. Therefore, when Dale had weekend visitation, there was no Summer. At least that was the agreement.

In actuality, in Dale's world there was nothing but Summer. And this was the second weekend we'd caught Dale, Summer, and little Jimmy spending, hopefully, for their sake, quality time together.

Two more weekends of photographing the separation agreement violation and we'll have earned our three grand and Judith will have gotten her proof to ball-bust the man who once was the love of her life.

I parked the car on the street. The wind was gusty and the

temp was in the mid-fifties with an overcast sky. Probably no dew to photograph. A few people were out and about. Joggers, walkers, a cyclist. A walker waved and said, "Good morning". I waved back.

With camera in hand, I walked up the drive which separated the two sets of quad homes. Dale Arneson's car was in the same spot where it was last night when I'd taken a picture of it with the house number. A look at the "V" indicated the vehicle hadn't moved. I took pictures of the "V", of the car and house number, and that's when I realized someone was in the car.

"Great, Harry," I said to myself. "You're slipping up in your old age."

How long had the person been there? Why hadn't he or she started the car? And why hadn't I noticed? Too doggone eager to take the pictures and skedaddle on back home. I took a closer look.

The person was a man sitting behind the wheel. And the man was Dale Arneson. He wasn't moving. He didn't see me, even though his eyes were wide open. My guess as to why he wasn't moving and didn't see me was that it had something to do with the fact the front of his shirt was very wet with what looked like blood.

———

Lieutenant Cal Swenson of Minneapolis Homicide, the same Cal Swenson who broke my sister's heart, had finished taking Bea's and my statements, told us he was working on trying to locate Tina, and said we were free to go. And go we did.

On the way back to home, sweet home, I decided to let the police break the news to our client that her husband was dead and her son, along with her husband's girlfriend, was missing.

The information wasn't something I wanted to give Judith Arneson at eight o'clock on a Sunday morning. Besides, I was just a wee bit pissed someone had stiffed us out of fifteen hundred bucks and felt my tax dollars needed to do some work. So let the Minneapolis police department tell Judith her kid's missing.

When we arrived at the little mansion on West Franklin, which we call home, there was a strange car parked at the curb and end of the walk to the front door. Bea stopped and I got out of her little Fiat. While she parked in the garage, I walked all around the machine that was a chunk of solidified liquid night. Bea joined me.

"What is it, Harry?"

"At first guess, I'd say it's a car."

She hit my arm. "Of course it's a car, silly. What kind of car?"

"An expensive one, is my guess."

"Like the Maserati I gave you, which you never drive?"

"Yeah. Kind of. Only I have a feeling this machine would make the price tag on the Maserati look like chump change."

I looked at the symbol but it didn't conjure up any automakers I was familiar with. My car's a Ford. Yes, Bea gave me the late Alicia Harris's Maserati. The late Alicia being Bea's former hife, which is a Tina-ism for the spouse in a same sex marriage. And Bea is right. I never drive the thing.

Rarely drive it is probably more accurate. Mostly because where I'm often required to go it's risky to drive a junker, let alone a car costing an eighth of a million bucks. Besides, I'm a Ford guy and I like my Focus wagon.

I do have to say one thing, though: in looking at the vehicle before me, no one at Ford could even dream of something like this. The machine parked at the curb was a creation of true exotic beauty.

The piece of sculpted midnight was unoccupied. I shrugged, took a look up and down the street, and concluded the car probably belonged to someone visiting one of our neighbors and the person was just rude enough to park the thing in front of our walk.

"Come on, Babe, let's go in and get some breakfast."

Holding hands, Bea and I walked up the walk to the house.

She had her key ready, unlocked the front door, and I pushed it open. Our noses took in the smell of bacon. Bea and I looked at each other and ran to the kitchen. There was Tina, cooking eggs and bacon. Buddy was sitting at her feet hoping for a handout, along with all three of her cats.

3

THE THIRD BARON LAKE

Late Sunday Morning. September 21st

WE HUGGED AND KISSED AND DANCED AROUND THE KITCHEN, UNTIL the eggs and bacon demanded attention. I poured orange juice. Bea made toast and when it was buttered, we went to the dining room to eat breakfast.

Bea blurted out, "Where were you? We were worried sick."

Tina finished chewing a bite of egg and swallowed. "Sorry. I needed time away and some space. I also had to do a favor for someone."

Bea pressed. "Where did you go?"

And I followed up, "Yeah, Sis. You can't disappear and not tell us something."

"All right. I'll give you the short version." She set down her fork and took a drink of orange juice. "When I left here, I drove to the airport and bought a ticket for Boston."

I interrupted. "And sent a text for us to pick up your car."

"Yes. Once in Boston, I booked a flight to Funchal, Madeira on British Airways via London. I had a thirteen hour layover and had to catch a bus from Heathrow to Gatwick. On the way to Gatwick, I booked a week's stay at The Cliff Bay in Funchal. Once there, I looked around and found a little place to rent for twenty-five dollars a night and took it for three months."

I found that to be a bit difficult to believe. "You mean no one else had booked it? That sounds odd."

"Yes. There were two other reservations for a week. I made it worth his while to cancel them."

I rolled my eyes. I didn't need to guess what her method of persuasion was. "He was single?"

"No. I didn't care. I wanted the place. He didn't care, either. He wanted the money and the tip."

"I see," I said. "The tip."

"I don't think I want to pursue this," Bea said.

Tina laughed. "Okay, Bea. Anyway, I got my room. Actually two rooms. A bedroom and a sitting room with a nice view of the ocean. No kitchen, although there was a hot plate and a few pots and pans. Oh, there was a bathroom and shower all in the space of a closet."

Bea wrinkled her nose.

"Once I settled in, I simply enjoyed the island. The food, the wine, the ocean. Mostly I enjoyed being alone. Then sometime towards the end of April, I met Russell Lake. Third Baron Lake. Very rich from commercial interests in Canada, mining interests in South Africa, and investments in the UK, US, Germany, and Russia."

"How rich is 'very rich'?" I asked.

"Oh, I don't know. Maybe somewhere around seven billion dollars. We had a very enjoyable time until he had to leave at the end of May. His present to me is out front. Had it shipped from England."

"That car is *yours*?" Bea and I chorused.

"Mm-hm. A Lamborghini Sesto Elemento. I think only twenty were made.

"When my time was up in my rooms, I rented a cottage. I wasn't ready to come back. The place was small, but it had a kitchen.

"In July, Russell came back and I spent a month cooking for him.

"Then my old boss cashed in on a favor he did for me. For six weeks I was back on the government's payroll and received an all expenses paid trip to the Ukraine. And that's all I can say.

"Now I'm home. I drove my car from New York to Minneapolis, stopping at the Cleveland and Chicago art museums along the way. Did you miss me?"

Bea and I both got up and hugged and kissed her.

"I missed you both. Dorothy was right."

————

The rest of the day was spent sitting by the fire, in the living room, chatting. We caught her up on what was happening around the Minneapple. Neither Bea nor I mentioned Cal and Tina didn't ask. I figure she's a big girl. Her love life is her business. What I know is she's home and it's good to have her back where she belongs. We didn't talk about business. I figured we can do that tomorrow. Once word is out she's back, the phone will start ringing and not stop.

4

HONESTY

Tuesday Morning. September 23rd

YESTERDAY WAS ABSOLUTELY GORGEOUS AND PASSED QUIETLY. THE high was in the low seventies and the sun was shining most of the time. A simply fabulous fall day and while Bea held down the fort, Tina drove her Lamborghini to her storage garage and I followed in the Focus. When we arrived, she parked her new baby next to her old one, a 1969 Alfa Romeo Spider Veloce.

"Nice car. How'd you talk him out of two and a half million dollars worth of automobile?"

"Relatively simple. I told him I very much enjoyed his company and would love to entertain him in Minneapolis and he wouldn't even have to give up his supermodel girlfriend. However, I wasn't cheap and I'd love to own a car like the Sesto Elemento. He balked, of course. I simply told him, 'I'm willing to play and have been playing — now you need to pay up. The piper must always be paid. And this piper can't be bought for a mere song.' He knew the jig was up and he parted with the car. I don't suppose I'll see him again."

She touched the Lamborghini tenderly, as a mother might her

newborn babe. "Men are a dime a dozen and there are only twenty of this car."

I was a little surprised at her callousness. We got into the Ford and I pointed the old station wagon in the direction of home.

"Tina, what you said sounds cynical even for you. Are you okay?"

"I'm fine, Harry. I did a lot of thinking while I was away. Cal threw me over for a two-bit bimbo. The Third Baron Lake thought he could buy a fuck buddy for dinner, drinks, and some interesting conversation. I thought a lot about what the late Reverend Mr. Barlow said regarding maintaining faith even if there never was a Jesus and I thought a lot about the retired Reverend Mrs. Barlow's blog posts arguing the opposite. We were raised in the faith. You threw it over in college."

I nodded.

"I never believed the organized church end of it, although I wanted some kind of faith in God and Jesus. However, Celeste's blog posts made me realize what I suppose I knew all along and what you also told me. No one needs religion or God to live a good life. They basically just need to follow the Golden Rule."

"Very true."

"The assignment I accepted in the Ukraine was routine. Although it wasn't without risk and things got a little testy for a few days. There, in that bleak and war-torn farmhouse, I decided I needed to live for me first. I need to be true to me. Because in the end I'm probably the only one who has my best interests listed as number one. You and Bea might have them pretty high, but only I have my interests as number one. Not even God or Jesus have my interests as number one. They have *their* interests as number one. My life is to honor them. My actions are to honor them. I said, 'To hell with that shit.' No, Harry, I'm looking out for me. I'm making sure *my* needs are met. First and foremost."

"Isn't that rather selfish?"

"All interest is self-interest, which I think you've emphasized a few times in the past. I'm just being honest with myself and you and the Third Baron Lake. And I'm okay with honesty. If others aren't, tough shit."

She lit a cigar and rolled the window down a couple inches. We drove on in silence. There really wasn't anything more to say. I didn't disagree with her. What I didn't like to hear was the position stated so baldly. Perhaps I'm still into self-deception.

Well, that was yesterday. Today, the phone started ringing early and Bea was certainly earning her pay answering it. And a good day it was for answering the phone and sitting at desks, because while the air was warm the sun went into hiding.

Tina was at her desk and I at mine. She was smoking a cigar and looking over reports of cases I'd worked on to get an idea of what we'd been up to and I was there to answer questions if she had any.

At half-past ten, or thereabouts, Bea came into the office. "There's a woman waiting to see you. I tried to make an appointment but she is insistent. She says she needs to see you now."

Tina put a frown on her face. Her cigar was only halfway finished and she never relights one. "Who is she?"

"Alex Brewer. She's campaign manager for Congresswoman Madelyn Horstman."

"I see." Tina looked over at the painting hanging above the fireplace. It was a flawless copy of a landscape scene by contemporary artist Art Pesso. Probably seeking inspiration from the wide open spaces depicted in the painting.

With a sigh, she said, "Give us five minutes and then send her in."

Tina extinguished the cigar and I opened windows and turned on the fan to make sure the cigar smoke didn't overpower our potential client. I also sprayed the room with Ozium to get rid of the cigar smell.

When the five minutes were up, Bea ushered in a tall woman, dressed in a gray suit which accentuated her masculine features. She had short brown hair. No glasses. A ring on her left hand. Bea made introductions and left. I was standing and indicated Alex

Brewer should sit in the oxblood oversized wingback. In spite of my use of the Ozium, I saw her wrinkle her nose.

Our visitor wasted no time. "Ms. Wright—" She hadn't listened to Bea's introduction.

Tina held up her hand, palm facing Brewer. "I am not a manuscript. MS is the abbreviation for a manuscript. I am an unmarried woman. The proper form of address is 'Miss'."

"So you're the submissive type."

I just barely stifled a guffaw.

"Not hardly," Tina said. "Call it advertising. When men learn I'm a Miss, they know I'm not married and available."

"Available for their control and manipulation."

Tina smiled. "Very few men have manipulated or controlled me, Manuscript Brewer. You, however, are like an open book." And Tina flashed her a "so there" smile.

"And I suppose you think 'gay' means 'happy'."

"It does. Aren't *you* happy, Manuscript Brewer?"

Brewer's eyes narrowed and the look she had on her face was meant to kill, if looks could do so. Then it was gone and she leaned back in the chair. *Miss* Wright, I am Congresswoman Madelyn Horstman's campaign manager. She requested I secure your services to help prevent an incident which could endanger her re-election chances and to find out who's passing secrets to Mark Aagard's campaign. For the record, I am opposed to hiring you, *Miss* Wright."

Tina shrugged. "Many people who don't want to come to me are, in the end, glad they did. You may end up one of them."

"I doubt it. Strange things do happen, though."

"What is this incident that needs preventing?"

"Mad's not popular within her party — are you a Democrat, Miss Wright?"

"I'm apolitical, Ms. Brewer. I rarely vote. It's a waste of time and energy and usually accomplishes little. Whoever is in office quickly succumbs to the lure of the lobbyist's money."

"I see. As I said, Mad's not popular with the party establishment. She bucks the old boys's club. She's progressive. Favors affirmative action for the LGBT community, is opposed to all voting restrictions, wants all gun manufacturing in the US stopped, wants an immediate cessation of all military action on the part of the US and a fifty percent reduction in the military, favors aggressive affirmative action for minorities in hiring so that they are favored over whites, supports Iran, and wants a mandatory Palestinian homeland created in Arab territory occupied by Israel. AIPAC has her in their sights. She narrowly defeated a primary challenge. The challenger, however, has not given up and while Simon Fishman is not openly helping Mark Aagard's campaign, he's doing what he can to sink Mad's."

"And what do you want me to do?"

"We want you to stop Fishman's behind the scenes smear campaign."

"What exactly is she being smeared with?"

"All manner of things. But the one she's most afraid of is a college indiscretion."

"Which was…?"

"She was a sugar baby for a couple years."

"And you think Fishman has this information?"

"We're positive he does."

"He told Mad, and I quote, 'I had a fruitful chat with an old college roommate of yours about how you paid for your college tuition and living expenses.' And then he told Mad to have a good day. Men." Brewer was quite steamed by the look she had on her face.

"But he hasn't used it yet," Tina said.

"No, he hasn't."

"And the information leak?"

"Yes. Someone in the campaign is leaking information to Aagard. We don't know who, but the person must be high up because of the nature of the information being leaked. We'd like the culprit found."

Tina leaned back in her chair and closed her eyes, softly drumming her fingers on the arm of her chair.

Brewer sat there looking at Tina. Didn't even favor me with so much as a glance. Probably because I was a despised member of that oppressive homophobic cabal of heterosexual men, whose sole purpose is to oppress women. Never mind I married a woman who was married to an abusive woman.

Tina opened her eyes and leaned forward.

"I want two hundred thousand dollars in cash. Hundreds and fifties are okay, although I would prefer smaller denominations. However, you might not have those on hand."

Brewer's mouth gaped. "We don't—"

"Of course you do. She's an incumbent Congresswoman. She has connections. If she's not worth millions by now, she soon will be. It's no secret Senators and Congressmen — and Congresswomen — use their knowledge of pending legislation to manipulate their investments and thereby make lots of money. Insider trading at its finest. In fact, the practice is such common knowledge it's been on TV for God's sake. If they aren't millionaires when they enter Congress, they soon are after they take the oath of office."

"You sure are cynical."

"Cynical my foot. Politics is about control. Control is about power. Power is about money and money is about power. That's how it's always been. Tell me when politics stopped being about control and power and money and I'll tell you that's when we discovered the moon was made of green cheese."

"Just a minute." Brewer took her smartphone out of a pocket and typed a message on it. Less than a minute later she had an answer. "Very well, Miss Wright, you'll have your money tomorrow. When will you start work?"

"As soon as I get the money."

"And you guarantee you'll stop the smear campaign and find our mole?"

"I guarantee I will get results. However, you may not like the results I get."

"What do you mean?"

"Maybe you or your assistant is the mole. Maybe her field director is the one sending a torpedo into the campaign. I only have what you've told me. People rarely tell the whole truth and nothing but the truth. Everyone of us is a liar."

"What a negative view of life."

"It's a realistic view. Don't tell me *you've* never lied."

Brewer just looked at Tina. Finally she said, "I don't like you. I'm going to tell Ms. Horstman not to hire you."

"Fine by me. When you walk out that door, I have a dozen potential clients to take your place. I don't need you. You, however, probably do need me."

Alex Brewer stood, turned around without so much as sullying her eyes on this member of the evil cabal of male oppressors, and left.

I got up and went out to the waiting room.

Bea said, "Alex was mad. Really mad."

"You know her?"

"Alicia did. Gave a big contribution to Madelyn Horstman's campaign when she first ran for Congress. I think she donated to her state senate campaign too. Alex has been with Madelyn for a long time."

"Interesting."

"Why was she mad?"

"Tina was too honest."

5

GARBAGE DISPOSAL

Tuesday Afternoon into Evening. September 23rd

FEINGOLD DROPPED IN SOMETIME DURING THE AFTERNOON FOR A FEW minutes. He's an attorney who has used Tina in the past to get evidence for him.

He talked for a minute or two about Celeste Barlow. Her case was the one which resulted in the rift with Cal. Feingold crowed how his legal skills had gotten her off with a year's probation and no fine.

Seems she's quit being a madam. Still has no interest in the church. Might become a Girl Scout leader.

On his way out, Feingold said, "Glad you're back, Miss Wright. Hope we can help each other out again soon. Very soon."

"You have my number, Mr. Feingold."

"That I do. That I do."

And he was gone.

The one who didn't show was Cal. Not that I expected him to do so. In fact, I'd say things will work out better for him if he stays away for awhile. Besides, he has a definite handicap: he doesn't own and certainly can't afford a Sesto Elemento.

Along about five, the doorbell rang. Bea and I were working

on supper, she'd decided to let the answering machine take the calls, and Tina was in the music room getting back in practice by playing Vaughan Williams's *Suite of Six Short Pieces* and *Six Teaching Pieces* on the piano. Bea went to the door and came back with a dozen red roses. Long stem.

As she passed through the kitchen, she whispered, "The note says they're from Cal." And on she went to the music room.

In no time at all, the "Slow Air" stopped in mid-note, Tina and said flowers marched into the kitchen, she turned on the cold water faucet, turned on the garbage disposal, and fed all twelve of those long-stemmed red 'American Beauty' roses to the disposal. When done, she shut off the disposal and water, returned to the music room and continued playing from where she left off.

Bea shook her head. "Wow. There's some emotion there."

I said, "Yep." And went back to the supper preparations.

When we sat down to eat, before wine was poured or food dished up, Tina glowered at Bea. "Next time, save me the bother. Either refuse delivery or throw them away yourself. That man is dead to me. If I could get away with it, I'd cut off his balls, shove them in his mouth, and then flay him alive."

"But Tina—"

Tina's hand went up, palm towards Bea. "Talk to the hand. On second thought, don't. I don't want to hold it up that long. Do not mention his name and do not defend him. Do I make myself clear?"

Bea nodded while looking at her plate. I almost burst out laughing. She looked for all the world as though she were five and being scolded by her mother. I didn't laugh, though. That was not the time to be laughing.

Supper passed with little conversation. Tina didn't seem to mind and when we were done eating, she went to the living room to smoke a cigar and drink a glass of Malmsey. Rather good Malmsey, too, it was. Blandy's 1996 Colheita. Fifty bucks a bottle. Bea and I joined her after we'd put the food away and washed the dishes. I opted for a glass of the wine, Bea passed. Nothing was said until Tina apologized.

"I'm sorry, Bea. I'm not ready to talk about him yet."

Bea nodded. "I understand."

"Forgive me?"

Bea got up, went to Tina, and kissed her. "Of course." Then she sat back down on the couch next to me.

Tina blew a stream of smoke towards the ceiling. "You know, we are very lucky to live in the United States. The Ukraine is rather primitive. And Western Europe isn't much better. Something so simple as a bathroom. Our bathrooms are so large and spacious. Hot water's rarely a problem. Even our poor are better off than most of the world's population. And we have the audacity to complain. We have problems but they are nothing compared to the rest of the world's."

What could we say to that? She's right. We are so wealthy here and we take it all for granted. I don't say, "America, love it or leave it." But I do ask folks to at least think twice before criticizing.

I wanted to bring up our potential client. Tina, however, doesn't like talking shop outside of the office, so I let the thought drop. Tomorrow would be soon enough. Two hundred grand, even in fifties and hundreds, wasn't going to be easy to come up with. I wonder if they'll even try.

6

IN THE MONEY

Wednesday Morning. September 24th

WE OFFICIALLY HAVE A CASE. ALEX BREWER CAME OVER AT TEN AFTER ten this morning and dropped off the money. Sacks and sacks of money.

I gave her a contract, which she signed, and told her I'd mail a receipt for the cash once Bea had finished counting what she'd given us.

Ms. Brewer also made it clear Tina was not her best friend.

"I was overruled," Alex said. "For some reason, Mad is hell-bent on having you investigate. So there you have it."

"Look at it this way, Ms. Brewer. The coach apparently wants me in the game. If you want to win, your personal feelings have to stay in the clubhouse. As do mine."

It was clear, at least to my eyes, Brewer didn't like what Tina was saying. She did, however, suck it up, and said, "You are right."

Tina was equally gracious. "Of course I am. Now, do you have a few minutes? I'd like to get some information."

"I can give you fifteen."

"Thank you. How long have you worked for the Congresswoman?"

"Ten years. I've managed all her campaigns."

"Where did you meet?"

"At a fundraiser for a Somali youth center. My wife is Somali. Ms. Horstman and I took to each other right away. She needed a campaign manager and I told her I could do it."

"Any idea who might be leaking information to the opponent's camp?"

"No. Whoever it is is very good."

"If a spy wants repeat business, he or she has to be good."

"I suppose so."

"I'd like a list of everyone working on the campaign."

"Paid staff and volunteers?"

"Yes. Everyone who is a regular."

"Define regular."

"Someone who consistently shows up to work, whether once a week or every day. The people you count on to be there."

"Okay. I can do that."

"If you have no idea who the mole might be, who don't you like?"

"Several people. I can note them on the list I send you."

"Please do so. And why are you not a suspect?"

"Me?" That question seemed to take Alex genuinely by surprise.

"Yes, you. This wouldn't be the first time a loyal servant betrayed his or her master or mistress."

"I suppose that is true. In my defense, let me say I believe in Mad. She's not only a friend, but her cause and mine are the same. I'm well paid for my services, but I'd work for free and did so on her first campaign. Money was tight back then. I love her and, if she was gay, I'd marry her. She's my best friend."

"Your hife is okay with this?"

"My hife?"

"Unfortunately, Ms. Brewer, the English language has not

caught up with contemporary pairings between and amongst people. I find hife to be a suitable term for the partners in a same sex marriage. It is a conflation between the words *husband* and *wife*, which are, as you know, gender specific. Hife is neutral. In fact, it would work for spouses in opposite sex marriages."

Brewer gave Tina a look that possibly indicated she doubted the Great Detective's qualifications for modifying the English language and then answered Tina's question. "Abba likes Mad, as well, and loves her children. I would not betray Congresswoman Horstman."

"What about Abba? She might like the Congresswoman and her children and not like your personal relationship with Madelyn Horstman."

"That's nonsense. Besides, Abba is not involved in the campaign. She'd have no access to information."

"What if she had a confederate?"

"Not possible. She talks to none of the campaign staff."

"That you know of."

Brewer gave Tina a look indicating she thought Tina wasn't playing with a full deck.

"In order for Harry and I to have access to the campaign staff, I'd like us to be security consultants."

"I'll let Damon Rossiter know. He'll get you badges. You can pick them up this afternoon. Come to the campaign headquarters and ask for Damon."

"Thank you for your time, Ms. Brewer."

Alex Brewer departed and Tina was left thinking. After a bit, I said, "Penny for your thoughts."

"Ask Bea to come here."

I got up and went to the outer office and retrieved my better half.

"You wanted to see me?" Bea took a seat on the chesterfield.

Tina nodded. "How well do you know Alex Brewer?"

"I don't actually know her. I was at a few parties or get-togethers, political stuff Alicia was involved in, and saw her there."

"What was your impression of her?"

"Calculating. Not very friendly. I've heard people say she has a temper. Rumor has it she used to drink, but stopped when she took up with Abba. Kind of a mean dry drunk, if you get what I mean."

"I do. Any other impressions?"

"Serious. Doesn't laugh much."

"Always about business?"

"Yeah. I'd say that."

"Thanks, Bea. That's been helpful."

Bea went back out to her desk in the outer office.

"Harry, I'd like you to go out to the campaign headquarters and get a feel for things. Go now and come back when you have some idea of what is going on out there."

"I'm off. I'll get our badges too."

I retrieved my hat and a sweater, kissed my sweetie goodbye, and took off for Eden Prairie. Nothing like wandering around a campaign headquarters to get a feel for the machinery and find out if it's well-oiled or heading for the ditch.

7

TURMOIL

Wednesday Afternoon. September 24th

I DECIDED A DETOUR TO THE LIBRARY WAS IN ORDER TO GIVE MYSELF A crash course on Madelyn Horstman's voting record, previous campaign platforms, and her troubles with the Democratic Party.

No sense going into the lion's den without info. I came away with two observations. First, I was glad she wasn't my representative. Second, her troubles within the party were being kept within the party. Save for the primary challenge from Simon Fishman.

If Fishman hadn't used the sugar baby info during the primary campaign, it was probably because he didn't have it. Which means if he has the dirt now, he got it after the primary campaign was over. That he hasn't used it yet, other than to threaten and bluster, could mean just about anything.

He could be negotiating with Aagard's campaign on a price. He could be simply holding on to the info to use whenever he thought the time was right. And all of this could be idle speculation, because Fishman might not even have the sugar baby info and is just pretending he does.

So he dropped a name. It doesn't necessarily mean he has any actual compromising information. Or it's a case of where Brewer thinks he has it and is the one yelling the sky is falling. Which begs the question, why does she think so?

From the library, I journeyed over to the White Castle in Nordeast, where they know me by name, for lunch and from there drove out to Horstman campaign headquarters, which is located in a ten story office building in beautiful Eden Prairie. Suite number 510.

The building itself was one of those sterile white piles of glass and concrete. It looked like a great big box. And sad to say, these monstrosities are like mushrooms: springing up everywhere new office buildings are to be found. You would think architects would get a bit creative.

I rode the elevator to the fifth floor. Number 510 was directly in front of me when the elevator doors opened. To my left was a corridor with numbers and arrows for the other five suites on the floor. The glass wall and door were plastered with campaign signs. One would have to be blind to miss Horstman's command center.

I stepped to the door and tried the knob. It turned and I pushed it open. Before me was a waiting area. There was a desk with a young woman sitting behind it. She wore a headset which was connected to her phone. Several plastic chairs lined the walls on my left and right. Otherwise, the look was Contemporary Sterile. I entered and walked to the desk.

The young woman was all smiles. "Welcome to Congresswoman Horstman's campaign headquarters. How may I help you?"

"My name is Harry Wright. Is Damon Rossiter available? I'm a consultant on campaign security."

"Is he expecting you, Mr. Wright?"

"I believe so. Alex Brewer told me to talk to him."

"One moment." She punched buttons on her phone and, in a moment, said, "Hi Damon. This is Opal at the reception desk. I have Harry Wright here. He said Alex told him to talk to you." There was a brief pause on her part. "Okay, fine."

She said, "Damon will be here in a moment."

I thanked her and took a seat, but didn't have a chance to get the chair warm when a young man entered.

"Are you Mr. Wright?"

I stood. "I am."

"Hi. I'm Damon Rossiter. Follow me."

I followed him through the door into a large room filled with tables and cubicles. Along the far wall were eight offices. He took me to the one on the far end. We entered and he closed the door.

"Have a seat." He took a seat behind the desk. I took one in front.

Rossiter was an average guy. Nothing stood out about him save for his pink necktie.

"So you're here to stop our internal leak."

"That's what I understand. My sister and I."

"Is she…?"

"Yes. She's that Justinia Wright."

He whistled. "I didn't know she did security work."

"Not per se. Industrial espionage, yes."

"I see. Okay. That fits. My thing is campaign security. Espionage isn't my gig. I've tried to see where we might have some leaks but so far I'm coming up with nothing."

"Then that means the mole is good and covers his or her tracks well. How is the campaign run?"

"Alex keeps a pretty firm hand on things. Every morning at eight we have a meeting—"

"Who's 'we'?"

"Oh. Mad, Alex, myself, Susan Wikstrom, Jawanda Clark, Prisca Thoraldson, Vi Nguyen, and Darius Littlewood."

"And they are?"

"Oh. Mad is—"

I held up my hand. "The others."

"Oh. Susan is the Field Director. Jawanda is our Communications Director, Prisca's in charge of fundraising, Vi is our legal beagle and makes sure we file all the right forms and stuff, and Darius is our IT guy."

"So all of you meet every morning."

"Right. If someone is not able to make it in person, they join us by Virtual Conference. It's like Skype."

"Who tends not to show up?"

"No one, really. The one most likely not to show up, is Mad. That's rare, though. Her district isn't that large. You know, the amount of ground it covers. So even if she has a meeting in an outlying area, she's usually back home afterwards. We're a dedicated group and Alex doesn't tolerate a lot of crap."

"Yet someone wants to sink the campaign."

"Yeah. That's pretty incredible. Everyone is so dedicated. At least it seems like it."

"If I understand what you're telling me, Alex runs a really tight ship. No dissension or independent thinking."

"Oh, my God. She's like Hitler."

"He didn't like gays."

Damon's face went blank.

"Hitler. He didn't like gays and lesbians. He was very middle class and conservative. Like the people who live in Ms. Horstman's district. The ones you want to vote for her."

"Oh. Really?"

"Yes."

He seemed at a loss. So I helped him out. "What goes on in your meetings?"

"Oh. Well, we talk about the campaign, give our reports and opinions, and then basically do what Alex tells us to do."

"What happens if someone disagrees?"

"With Alex?"

I nodded.

"It's best if you don't. Not unless you want your balls busted."

I filed the information away. A good model for our democratic republic. I changed the subject. "You have our badges?"

"Sure do. Right here." He pushed two name tags across to me."

"No pictures?"

"No. We aren't that sophisticated. Besides, Mad's big on trust. Gotta trust people. Believe in their good intentions."

"I see." I almost tweaked him and then decided why bother. I put on my badge and pocketed Tina's. "Mind if I look around?"

"No, not at all. If you need me, I'll be here. I'm working on Mad's schedule."

"One more thing. How long have you worked for Mad?"

"I came on board last year. Darius, too."

"What happened to the person before you?"

"I understand she quit. Got into a fight with Alex."

"Thanks."

"Oh, don't mention it."

I got up and left the office, closing the door behind me. There wasn't much activity. The sterile white walls were covered with campaign signs and pictures of the congresswoman.

"This place gets really hopping at night."

I turned and saw a pretty smile on an equally pretty young Asian woman.

She looked at my name tag. "Oh, so you're one of the consultants. Hi. I'm Vi." She stuck out her hand which I took and shook. "I'm the campaign's lawyer."

"Hi. I'm Harry Wright."

"Pleased to meet you. You going to be around awhile?"

"For awhile."

"Come on in. Let's talk."

Vi's office was two doors down from Damon's. I noticed the office in between had the name of Prisca Thoraldson stuck on the door. I walked into Vi's office and she closed the door. She sat at her desk and indicated a chair along the side wall. She turned to face me.

"Your boss really pissed off Alex."

"Is that so?"

"Yep. Alex was adamantly opposed to hiring her. Mad insisted, however. Honestly, I'm surprised. Alex usually gets her way.

"Really?"

"Mm-hm. She runs the show pretty much."

"Is Alex liked?"

Vi burst out laughing. "Sorry. No. I don't think anyone *likes* Alex. Respect, maybe. Perhaps even admire. But like? No."

"Why don't you like her?"

"When I started working here, she hit on me. I told her I don't swing that way. She wouldn't take 'no' for an answer. Finally, I threatened to go to Mad."

"That stopped it?"

"Yes. But then she was cold and even a little mean. She doesn't like to be thwarted. She's basically a despot and not very benevolent. I don't like those kind of people."

"Others have the same complaint? About being hit on?"

"Not the guys. She just hates them. The women? Yeah. She hits on most of them. Even some who are married."

"She get any takers?"

"Some."

"Her wife know?"

"Not sure Abba would say anything if she did."

"I see. Congresswoman Horstman must like her. Alex, that is."

Vi thought a moment. "I guess she does at that."

"Any idea who might be the mole?"

"Take your pick. The people here love Mad. There are some who really hate Alex and they, at least some of them, might be willing to throw Mad under the bus just to get at Alex."

"And who might these people be?"

"Susan Wikstrom and her assistant, Ross Felder. Prisca Thoraldson had a big argument with Alex. Went so far as to call her a 'fucking dyke bitch' right out there on the floor. She almost got the boot."

"What stopped her from getting it?"

"I think she threatened to sabotage the fundraising list. Of course the guys have had run-ins, Damon and Darius. But being a guy automatically gets you on Alex's hate list. The only way to avoid trouble, if you're a guy, is to basically just say yes to whatever she wants and never question her. She also pissed off a big contributor. That took a lot of sweet talking on Mad's part and an apology by Alex."

"Who's the contributor?"

"Yolanda Gomez."

I shook my head. "Seems like the campaign has a lot of inner turmoil."

"It does. And almost all of it goes back to Alex."

"Were previous campaigns like this?"

"Don't know. Wasn't here."

"How long have you been here?"

"Just a year. My predecessor got a job in some think tank. At least that is what I heard."

"This has been very enlightening, Vi."

"Glad I could be of help."

"How about you?"

"What about me?"

"You didn't include your name on your list. So I take it you aren't a suspect."

She gave me a great big charming smile. "No, I didn't include myself. But that was *my* list. Ask some others and see whose names you get."

"I'll do that. I'll let you know if you show up on any."

"No need. I'm sure I will."

I thanked her for taking the time to talk to me and walked out onto the floor.

Odd. So very odd. The people here love the Congresswoman and hate the campaign manager.

Mad and Alex seem to be friends, yet seem so different in their personalities. Unless it is a case of birds of a feather. In which case, Mad might turn out to be a real asshole. It might also be a case of the Congresswoman being the good cop. And as we all know, cops are, well, cops.

My watch told me the time was half-past three. Jawanda Clark's and Darius Littlewood's offices were dark. Alex was in her office and so was Susan Wikstrom. I decided to see what, if anything, Susan might have to say. Her door was open and I poked my head in.

"I'm Harry Wright. One of the special consultants—"

"I know who you are, Mr. Wright. Unfortunately, I'm busy right now and can't talk with you." She hadn't even taken her eyes off of her computer screen.

"Maybe later?"

"Probably not." She looked at me. "The problem is Alex Brewer. I've told Mad to get rid of her. Mad refuses to listen to reason. Whatever happens, happens. I'll get another job if Mad loses. Unfortunately, Mad will come back to Minnesota and a promising career will go down the toilet. She'll be a nobody, which ought to make her husband quite happy. Now, if you'll excuse me."

"Thank you for the information. Hope you have a better day."

She didn't respond. Her face was once again directed to the computer screen.

Very interesting the dynamic in this place. I noticed a young man sitting at a desk in a cube. A name card identified him as Ross Felder, Assistant Field Director. Hm. Maybe he had time to talk. I walked over to the cube and knocked on the metal molding strip.

"Sorry. Can't talk. I'm leaving." He spoke to the computer screen, although I assumed he was talking to me. He looked up. "Who are you?"

I pointed to the name badge. "Harry Wright. Security consultant."

"Oh. I suppose you want to talk about the leak. Sorry. I'm leaving. Have a meeting with a printer. Best to make an appointment." He threw on a jacket and took off.

Busy, busy, busy. Or else they don't really want to talk. Could be both, of course. Then again, perhaps, like Brewer, Wikstrom and Felder hadn't wanted to hire us and what I was running into was passive aggressive behavior.

I took another look around the large room. Forty-one days to the election. All the discord. All the suspicion. All the distrust. None of it bode well for a victory lap in November.

The slogan on the white board caught my eye. Perhaps it was the motto for the day. "Feel Their Pain". Appropriate. Very appropriate.

8

UNEXPECTED GUESTS

Wednesday Night. September 24th

WHEN I GOT HOME, I REPORTED TO TINA WHAT I'D LEARNED.

"Thanks, Harry. Brewer faxed over the list of staffers. There's a breakdown of the paid staff, the names of the regular volunteers, about two dozen of them, and then a call list of about five dozen names. Brewer noted her suspicions. Top of the list is Thoraldson, followed by Wikstrom and Felder. There are three of the regular volunteers she doesn't trust, which we can add to the list. I'd like to talk to Wikstrom and Felder as soon as possible."

"I'll see what I can do."

"I'm going to play the piano for awhile. I have a headache."

Tina departed and I was right behind her. My destination, however, was the kitchen.

Bea and I made supper, while listening to Philip Glass's minimalist piano music on the iPod. The evening meal was spaghetti and salad, with a delicious California Petite Syrah to accompany the food. Afterwards, we all sat in the living room drinking tea and eating apple pie.

Along about eight, tea and pie finished off, the doorbell rang. I went to see who it was. Through the peephole I saw a youngish woman standing on our porch. I opened the door and asked how I could help her.

"My name is Jawanda Clark. I'm Congresswoman Horstman's Communications Director. May I talk with Justinia Wright?"

"Come in. Wait here, please, and let me see if she's available."

I went to the living room. "Horstman's Communications Director would like to talk with you."

Tina's face took on the look of one sorely inconvenienced.

"You going to talk to her?"

She sighed. "I suppose."

"Can I listen in?" Bea asked.

"You may," Tina responded.

The three of us headed for the office, picked up Ms. Clark along the way, made introductions, and got ourselves comfortably situated in the Inner Sanctum.

Tina and I at our desks, Bea on the chesterfield, and Jawanda in the oversized oxblood wingback.

"How may I help you, Ms. Clark?"

"I understand you are trying to find out who is leaking information to Aagard's campaign."

"That is what I was hired to do, yes," Tina responded.

"I think I may be able to help you."

"Okay."

"I think it's Prisca Thoraldson. She's the one leaking the information."

"And why do you think she's passing information to the Congresswoman's opponent?"

"She had a big fight with Alex Brewer several months back and almost got fired over it. But she told Alex and Mad in no uncertain terms she'd make sure they wouldn't have a single donor left if they let her go."

"So she blackmailed them into keeping her."

"Yes."

"Having kept her job, why would she now try to sink the campaign?"

"Because donations have fallen off and Alex is pushing for her to be replaced."

"Is she still threatening to poison the donors?"

"Probably, but with donations falling off the threat isn't as effective."

Tina pursed her lips and nodded. "Why does the Congress-woman keep Ms. Brewer? She seems to be a divisive element in the campaign."

"They're friends and there is some talk they might be lovers."

"The Congresswoman is married."

"It's no secret her husband isn't happy with her being in Washington."

Tina raised her eyebrows, leaned back, and rested her chin on steepled fingers. "What is his role in the campaign?"

"He doesn't have much of one. He is around and appears with the Congresswoman. That's about it."

"How does he interact with the staff and volunteers?"

"Oh, he's very friendly with everyone. He's not opposed to her being in office. He'd just like it to be local, here in the state."

"Do you have any evidence Ms. Thoraldson is betraying the campaign?"

"One of my staffers overheard part of a phone conversation which led her to believe Prisca was going to meet with someone and talk about the campaign."

"When was this?"

"Two months ago."

"Did you tell anyone?"

"No."

"Why not?"

"With the campaign having problems and my person not hearing the whole thing, I thought it best not to create more problems."

"So why now?"

"The situation is no better and we need help. We desperately need help."

"Who is the person who overheard the phone conversation?"

"Her name is LaQueesha Washington."

"And what does she do on the campaign?"

"She's a volunteer. Really good at her job. She writes up press releases."

"How long has she been with the campaign?"

Jawanda sat back in the chair and thought a moment. "I think she's been with Mad for at least a couple campaigns. Has done all manner of jobs. Whatever needs to be done. I kind of appropriated her this time around."

"How long have you been with the Congresswoman?"

"A little over four years."

"How well do you get along with Alex Brewer?"

"Well enough. I know that there is no sense in questioning her directly. If I disagree, I talk direct with Mad."

Tina chewed on that piece of information for a bit. From my perspective, it seemed Jawanda had discovered the key to successfully navigating Horstman campaign politics. The internal kind.

"Anything else, Ms. Clark?"

"No. Just wanted to let you know what I'd heard."

"Thank you for the information."

"You won't tell anyone where you got it from, will you?"

"Will that be a problem?"

"Might be if Alex finds out."

"I'll do my best to keep it quiet."

"Thank you so much."

Jawanda Clark stood and I walked her to the door and bid her a goodnight. When I returned, Tina was staring at the back wall with a scowl on her face.

I sat at my desk. "What's that look for?"

"I'm going to have to up my fee to a half-million. Maybe then they'll go away."

Rather innocently, Bea asked, "If you have no clients, how can you stay in business?"

The scowl transferred to Bea. "Maybe if I charged more, I'd get better clients."

I saw my opportunity and took it. "What she's saying, Babe, is this: she only wants clients who pay her money and don't ask her to work."

Tina glared at me.

"Or maybe, Sis, you could become a personal coach, charge a hundred a half-hour, and help your client decide if he or she wants to go to a movie or stay at home and stream one. Obviously, a deciding factor is theater popcorn versus homemade. You could—"

"Harry, shut up. That campaign is like the *Titanic*. And even if there were enough lifeboats for everyone, that isn't stopping the ship from sinking. They're doomed. And given their penchant for suicide, they might even drill holes in the lifeboats."

"Maybe," I said. "Nevertheless, you took their money and you need to deliver something."

A scowl joined the glare on her face. Don't know how she does that.

"Hey. You move that face elsewhere. I'm not the one who said yes."

Bea started giggling. "You two—" She couldn't get anymore out.

The scowl and glare disappeared and a hint of a smile replaced it. "I suppose you'd best get Prisca here, Harry. She's a lead and we need to follow up. We also need to talk to this LaQueesha and find out what she heard."

"Okay, will do."

"I think we probably need to talk to Horstman and her husband. Why does she tolerate the chaos? If the Mister doesn't want her in Washington, might he actually work against her? I think we need to talk to them tomorrow. Harry, you see the husband and I'll see the wife."

"Sounds good. I'll get Thoraldson here as soon as possible."

I counted fingers. Seven people I had to call and convince they needed to speak with the Great Detective. If anyone deserved to have a scowl on his face, it was me.

The doorbell rang. The time was quarter to ten.

The scowl reappeared on Tina's face and I let her have it. At least for the time being. I went to the door. This time a man was standing on our porch. He was of medium height and build, with a bit of a paunch. I opened the door to the length of the chain.

"How can I help you?"

"I'd like to see Justinia Wright."

"What about?"

"I'm Jim Oberman. I'm with Mark Aagard's campaign. I have a proposition for Ms. Wright."

"You better call her Miss Wright or she'll drop kick you right through the goalpost. Come on in."

I escorted him into the Inner Sanctum, made introductions, and directed him to sit in the oversized oxblood wingback.

Oberman looked around the office and was about to say something when Tina cut him off.

"It's late, Mr. Oberman, what do you want?"

"As I told your assistant, I have a proposition for you."

"What is it?"

"I'm Mr. Aagard's Communications Director. We've learned you've been hired by Congresswoman Horstman."

"Okay. You've heard that."

"We'd like to hire you, as well."

"What's your proposal?"

"We want you to obtain a piece of information for us."

"What information and who has it?"

"The information is in the hands of Simon Fishman. He ran—"

Tina held up her hand. "I know about him. What does he have that you want and can't get from him?"

"He has a recording of a young woman which compromises the character of the Congresswoman. We've made him a fair offer. However, he won't sell. Wants more money."

"That's simple. Give him what he's asking."

"We were hoping—"

"Hoping what?"

"Hoping you'd get the recording for us."

"Why would he sell it to me?"

"Not sell…"

"Mr. Oberman, I'm not a professional thief. I am a professional private detective. I'm sorry, but I can't help you. As long as you're here, maybe you can help me."

"What do you want to know?"

"Who's passing information to you or your candidate from the Congresswoman's campaign committee?"

"Sorry. Can't help you."

"Can't or won't?"

"You scratch my back…"

"Fifty thousand to you if you give me the name of the person along with proof."

The wheels were turning in Oberman's head. They didn't turn for very long though.

"Make it—"

"No deal. Fifty thousand or nothing. I will get the information. I was just hoping to save time by getting it from you."

"Cash?"

"Of course, cash. That way we can both deny it if we so choose."

"I'll see what I can find out. I'll be in touch." He stood. "Good-night, Miss Wright."

"Goodnight, Mr. Oberman."

I escorted our visitor back out into the Minnesota fall night. The air was quite crisp. I took in a big lungful before closing the door.

Back in the Inner Sanctum, Bea was talking. "…politics was so dirty."

"Of course, it's dirty," Tina said. "After all, it's about power and power is the most addictive drug there is. People have killed to gain power or keep it."

"I guess, but right here in America?"

"Why do you think people are any different here than elsewhere? Read *All the Kings Men*. It will open your eyes. Well, Harry, what do you think?"

"I think it's time to go to bed." I didn't bother stifling the yawn.

"I suppose it is. Busy day tomorrow. Given what I know now about this case, I should have asked for more money."

To Bea, I said, "Power. Makes one greedy."

"Harry, shut up."

9

STAND UP

Thursday Morning. September 25th

NOTHING WAS OUT OF THE ORDINARY IN OUR BREAKFAST RITUAL THIS morning. Tea and orange juice, toast and jam, pastries and muffins on the table. Bea and I reading the newspaper. Tina, nose in her iPad, after reminding us to wash hands.

Manly was chasing Buddy or Buddy, Manly. Isis was in Tina's lap and Prudy was in mine. So when the doorbell rang at a few minutes before nine we sat there looking at each other. Finally I said I'd get it.

Through the peephole, I saw a blond woman in her upper twenties or early thirties on our porch. I opened the door.

"Sorry to call so early in the morning. Is Justinia Wright available?"

"And you are?"

"Prisca Thoraldson."

I'd love to take the credit for having Ms. Thoraldson show up without my even phoning her, but I doubt anyone would buy it. I invited her in and had her sit in our waiting room, then returned to the dining room.

"Prisca Thoraldson wishes to talk to you, Tina."

She glared at me.

"Nope. I haven't even phoned her."

Tina let out a "humph" and after a moment sighed. "Bring all this to the office. I'm going to have my breakfast." She stood and walked out of the dining room. I also did a "humph" because Tina barely eats anything for breakfast. This was pure show.

Bea and I put the food and teapot on a couple trays and took them to the Inner Sanctum, where Tina was sitting behind her desk and Prisca was in the oxblood wingback.

I offered tea and juice to our guest, she took juice. Bea offered her a choice of pastries, muffins, or toast. Our guest took a muffin. The rest of us took tea and pastries. Bea sat on the chesterfield and I at my desk.

"Sorry to interrupt your breakfast. This was the only time I had available today. I want to know what you've heard about me." Prisca took a sip of juice and then a bite of muffin.

Tina dabbed a napkin to her mouth. "What makes you think we've heard anything?"

"Because I know Alex."

"We've heard the two of you don't get along."

"That's an understatement. And, no, we don't get along."

"How long have you worked for Madelyn Horstman."

"Three years."

"Why don't you and Ms. Brewer get along?"

"Personality clash."

"When did that start?"

"Day two or three after I started."

"Why are you passing information to Aagard's campaign?"

"I'm not."

"Who is?"

"I don't know." She looked at her watch. "I'm going to have to go. I have a meeting with a potentially big donor."

"Very well. A good day to you."

"Thanks. I need it. The person who needs to go, the one causing all of the problems is Alex. When Mad wins this, I'm done. I'm not working with Brewer any longer than I have to." She stood and Bea escorted her out.

Tina had a frown on her face.

"What's that for?"

"Manners. Didn't even thank us for the juice and muffin and then didn't even finish it."

I shook my head. "Some people's kids."

"Go ahead and make fun. It's why there are all these shootings. No manners. No respect. No gratitude."

What could I say? She was probably right.

Bea returned. "That's one less thing on your list, Harry. How did you work that?"

"Must be my powers of mental telepathy."

Tina, with a bite of kolache in her mouth, said, "Work your powers and get Ms. Horstman here."

"I'll try Boss. I know how you hate to expend energy working here, let alone not here."

"You're considerate of your little sister, Big Brother."

"You're the only sister I have." And I blew her a kiss.

Bea was giggling. "You two are so funny."

I pressed on, "What do you think, Tina, should I try stand up?"

"I think the only stand up you're going to be doing is standing up to go to your car to interview Horstman's husband."

"Shoot. I thought the Harry and Tina show might help us through the slow times."

"Take my brother… Please."

"Ha. Ha. Very funny."

"What's your problem? You're the one who wanted to do stand up."

"I've moved on."

Tina winked at Bea, put her hand to her mouth, and in a stage whisper said, "Got him."

Bea giggled and I put in a call to Alex Brewer.

10

TED TALKS

Ms. Brewer gave me the phone numbers for both Horstmans. I passed Madelyn's to Tina and called Mr. Horstman, whose given name I learned was Theodore. I was also advised to call him Ted.

On the second ring, Ted answered and we set up a one o'clock meeting at a restaurant out in Plymouth.

To pass the time until our appointment, I did some looking online to see what I could find out about him.

He is owner of a cleaning company called Clean Sweep, which provides cleaning services to businesses. Revenues are over eleven million a year. The company has thirty-five employees. His salary is half a mil a year. Not huge. Nothing to sneeze at either.

He's forty years old and was born in Minnesota. I found a few pictures of him on the internet which should help me to identify him at the restaurant.

In addition to finding info on Ted, I called Jawanda Clark and got the number for LaQueesha Washington and when she didn't answer, left a message.

Along about noon, with another beautiful fall day making the Land of Ten Thousand Lakes a nice place to live, I fired up the

Maserati and drove out to Plymouth. This was one of those very rare times when I decided to drive the car.

Part of the problem is the thing costs beaucoup bucks. At least a hundred grand to replace, should I want to replace it. Today, seeing as I was going to Plymouth, which is far from a seedy part of town, I thought it would be safe to park and not have to be afraid of something happening to it.

Also, in case I have to tail Mr. Horstman, it's best if he not see me in my Focus wagon.

And just in case he had a desire to brag about cars, well, I had one I could brag about right along with him.

Traffic was heavy on I-394 and I-494. Lots of trucks moving goods, keeping our economy strong and healthy. Lots of cars, too. I can understand the trucks. Those are people working. But the cars? I always ask myself when I'm out and about what are all these people doing on the freeway during the middle of the day. Don't they work?

Someday, when I have nothing better to do, I might follow one and see what it is he or she is up to. On the other hand, maybe I don't actually want to know.

The lot at Al's Place had parking spots to spare. I was early and found a place to park far enough away from the doors to let me observe both the entrance and most of the lot. A couple minutes before one a car entered.

I watched it circle around and park not far from the front doors. A BMW 24 Roadster. Nice car. Not as nice as my Maserati, but certainly nicer than my Focus. I gave him a couple minutes and then followed him in.

The interior was done up in pseudo-rustic. Dark. Fake wood beams. Fireplace. I didn't see him and mentioned to the hostess I was meeting someone for lunch. She was all smiles, her blouse was unbuttoned enough to reveal plenty of cleavage, and her backside did plenty of undulating in the tight skirt as I followed her to his table. I thanked her and, still smiling, she left.

"Ted Horstman? I'm Harry Wright."

"Hi, Harry. Have any trouble finding the place?"

"No. Just traffic."

"Yeah, it's a bear."

The server arrived, announced her name was Lizzie, put menus on the table, and asked what we'd like to drink. Ted ordered a draft Grain Belt and I, the house red wine. I noticed she too was fairly well endowed.

"Ever eat here, Harry?"

"No."

"Steaks are great."

I looked at the menu. It was heavy on the beef. Kind of a macho man's menu. Which probably accounted for the cleavage and the endowment. I decided on a hamburger.

Our drinks came, Lizzie took our orders, and departed. Ted went with steak and potatoes. A real down home Minnesota middle-class kind of meal.

He took a sip of beer. "So what can I help you with?"

"What's your role in your wife's campaign?"

"Don't really have one. Mostly I just stand by her side and smile."

"What about when she is in Washington?"

"Look, Harry, I have a business to run." He drank beer. "This politics stuff is Maddie's. I'd rather she was here in Minnesota. I don't like her being in Washington." He drank beer. "Not a good crowd there."

I sipped my wine. It was okay. A typically nondescript house wine. "So why do you let her? Or do you?"

He smiled. "This is something Maddie really wants. No use trying to stop her. It's like hitting your head against a wall. It feels good when you stop. I stopped. Get my drift?"

"I do." I sipped wine and he polished off his beer. "So you don't interfere with her political ambitions and you have peace."

"That about says it all."

"Have kids?"

He nodded and signaled the server for another beer.

"So you run the business and take care of the kids and she helps run the country."

"You got it."

"The campaign seems to be in a lot of turmoil. Is that SOP?"

"Standard Operating Procedure?"

I nodded and sipped wine, he got his beer and salad.

"Well, yes and no. Yes, in that few campaigns ever run like a well oiled machine. No, in that for some reason this campaign isn't going well for Maddie. Lots of personality clashes with that Brewer woman."

"What do you think of Alex Brewer?"

"She's a man-hating dyke, that one. Have no idea what Maddie sees in her. They're friends, though, and Alex seems to know what she's doing. Although the recent staff changes aren't working out well."

"Who's new?"

"I'm not really the one to ask. I think that lawyer is new. The security and IT guys are also new. Beyond that, you'll have to ask Alex."

"I take it you don't get along with Alex Brewer."

"I'm a man. That's four strikes against me right there."

"I see."

Our meals came and we talked a bit about the food and then the conversation segued to sports and finally I got it back to the campaign.

"Why do you think someone would want to sabotage the campaign? Everyone seems to think your wife is fabulous."

"Have no clue. My guess is it all goes back to Alex. There's just too much bad chemistry. I think she pissed someone off and that person is going to sink the campaign to teach her a lesson. No facts. Just a guess."

"And no idea who that might be?"

"Nope. Hope you find who it is soon, otherwise Maddie's going to be an unemployed politician."

When the check came I let him pay for it after making an offer.

He insisted. Either way, it wasn't coming out of my pocket. I thanked him for lunch and the information.

"Sorry I couldn't have been of more help, Harry."

"No need to apologize. You've been plenty helpful."

"Well, if you think so."

"I do."

We shook hands and he went to his car and I mine. When I got to the Maserati, I saw him sitting in his car talking on his cell.

Of course that piqued my interest. Who could he be talking to? Someone on the campaign? Someone at the office?

I got into my car.

He and the missus had talked about her congressional run. He didn't want her in Congress. He wanted her home. But there she was in Congress. In Washington. Obviously he'd lost and had decided to quit hitting his head against the wall.

What if instead of taking on that wall again, he decided to bore a hole in the Congressional ship of state? Possible. Was it probable? That was the question. And the answer lay in how badly Ted Horstman wanted Madelyn Horstman by his side right here in the Land of Ten Thousand Lakes.

After Horstman drove off, I decided to drive the fifteen miles down to Eden Prairie and check in at the campaign headquarters. Since I was in the neighborhood, so to speak.

The traffic was starting to get heavy on the freeway. Even so, it wasn't heavy enough to stop me from doing my man thing putting the Maserati through its paces. Those fifteen miles blew by in eleven and a half minutes. Thank who or whatever runs the universe the state troopers were patrolling elsewhere.

At the headquarters, most everyone was there. Notable exceptions were Prisca Thoraldson, Damon Rossiter, Alex Brewer, and, of course, the Congresswoman. I made a beeline to Wikstrom's office.

Before a word came out of my mouth, she said, "You again."

"Yep. Me again. Let's face it, Ms. Wikstrom, we're going to talk."

"Not now. I'm busy."

"How about tonight? My sister's place. She'd love to talk to you, too."

"No. I'm busy."

I took out my smartphone and started talking loud enough so she could hear, even though I was only addressing myself. "Let me see. Madelyn Horstman. Ah, here's her number."

"What do you want, Mr. Wright?"

"I told you. A chat. Actually, it's more my sister wants to chat and tonight would be just great. You could even bring your assistant. The more the merrier."

She sighed. "What time?"

"Eight. Nine. Whatever works best for you. I know you're busy."

She was looking at me and the only thing missing was her tongue sticking out at me.

"See you tonight, then?"

"Yes, Mr. Wright, we'll see you tonight."

"Great! Well, I'll shove off now. Seeing that you're very busy." I put a business card on her desk, right in front of her. "Not difficult to find. Call if you need directions."

"I have GPS. Now, if you don't mind, I have work to do."

"I'm sure you do. Ciao." And I left making a buzzing sound like that of bees.

Mission accomplished, the time had come to head home and apprise the Great Detective of my coup. And by the looks of things, I'd probably need to set up the portable bar.

11

TINA'S INTERVIEWS

Thursday Evening. September 25th

Tina wasn't home when I got back. Bea said she was meeting the Congresswoman at a bar in northeast Minneapolis.

The hour was inching its way to mealtime, however I wasn't ready to tackle that chore. Instead, I built a fire in the office fireplace. Once I had it going, I stretched out on the couch and thought about the case.

Thus far we were nowhere. A few fingers pointed to Prisca, implicating her as being the source of the leak. Her own statement, that she was going to leave after the campaign was over, told me the possibility was strong she was not heavily invested in the campaign, regardless of the outcome.

Did that necessarily mean she would purposely betray her candidate? No, it did not. The fight was with Alex, not Madelyn.

No one we've talked to thus far has anything against the Congresswoman. What the situation was beginning to look like was that Madelyn Horstman's political career was going to end up being collateral damage in the war between the campaign manager and the staffers.

The only person associated with Madelyn who didn't want her

in Washington was her husband. It seemed to me we needed to find out how badly he wanted her home. Badly enough to sink her campaign?

I had dozed off somewhere in my ruminations and was awakened by Tina kissing my forehead.

"Hey, Tina. How did your meeting go with the Congresswoman?"

"Fine, if you like talking to self-important stuffed shirts. God, a typical leftist prig. Is Bea making supper?" She sat at her desk, poured herself a glass of madeira, and fired up a cigar.

"She wasn't in the outer office?"

"No."

"Then she must be preparing our evening victuals. Did you record the interview?"

"I did. Not sure it will provide us with anything more than my memory will. Basically, Horstman is at a complete loss why someone would want to betray her."

"I assume you pointed out Brewer as the problem."

"I did. Her reaction was Alex can do little wrong." Tina began mimicking the Congresswoman. "I know Alex can be a bit head-strong and sometimes rubs people the wrong way, but she's a lovely person. I just love her. Don't know where I'd be without her." Tina rolled her eyes.

"Head in the clouds?"

"Head up her ass is more like it. She's far more concerned about Fishman dropping the sugar baby bomb."

"Does he actually have the information?"

"Apparently he does. He played her a portion of the recording. The voice was that of a former college roommate."

"He's blackmailing her."

Tina sent a cloud of smoke towards the ceiling. "Uh-huh. To the tune of two hundred and fifty thousand dollars."

"Wow. That's going to bleed the campaign. Especially after what you charged them."

She sent a perturbed look my direction. "That's what Madelyn thinks: that he wants to siphon off enough cash to financially cripple the campaign."

"A campaign with no money is essentially no campaign." I decided to pour myself a glass of Sercial madeira. And we had a fine five year old Cossart Gordon on hand.

"Certainly in this day and age. No money, no campaign. He'll suck her dry and those vital last minute commercials and mailers won't see the light of day."

"Who knows about her being a sugar baby?"

She took a sip of madeira. "Her former roommate, who Fishman found. Otherwise, no one on the campaign, except for Alex. Not even her husband knows and that worries the Congresswoman. She's afraid he might leave her. Or even worse, force her to give up the campaign."

"Aside from the husband, is this actually such a big deal?"

"She seems to think so."

I shook my head. "All this worry is crazy if you ask me. So what if word got out. She could just blow it off. The whole thing took place years ago. Who'd care? And if Fishman dropped the bomb, all Horstman has to do is to go before the cameras, with her husband beside her, and make some promise to increase college money so women wouldn't have to do such things."

"Assuming he'd stand beside her." She sent a cloud of smoke towards the ceiling. "I know. Doesn't make sense. But she's worried about her image because she's taken such a strong public stand against prostitution and porn. They demean women. It's male lust making sex objects of women."

"Yeah, but not all sugar babies have sex with the guys. Sometimes it's just meeting for coffee at Starbucks or Caribou."

"And you know this how?"

"Very funny. I read, Sis."

"Uh-huh."

"You don't pay me enough to have a sugar baby."

"Good thing too. Otherwise I'd have Bea to deal with."

I rolled my eyes. "Anyway, I suppose there are those people

who probably don't see it that way. They're probably the ones
with money. Or there might be those who'd say, 'Oh, she can do it
and we can't.'"

"Right. It's okay she pimped herself to go to college, but no
other young woman should. A touch of hypocrisy there."

I smiled. "Yeah. So in the end, you didn't get much."

"Not really. Did you get anything out of the husband?"

"Some." I went on to tell her what Ted Horstman and I talked
about.

When I was done, she sat back in her chair, chin resting on
steepled fingers. She sat that way for three or four minutes before
speaking.

"Harry, we need to find the roommate and either get her to
retract her statement or discredit her. The second thing we need to
do is find out how badly Ted Horstman doesn't want his wife in
Congress. And number three is to talk to the rest of the staffers."

"Horstman will be easy. All we have to do is talk to people
since he isn't keeping his dislike a secret. I have a call in to LaQueesha and Wikstrom and Felder are stopping by tonight. What
about the roommate?"

"That's where the problem lies. We have her maiden name,
Tricia Long, and that's all. Horstman has no idea where she's
living or if she's married."

I thought about that. For starters, how many Tricia Longs
might there be? And then what if she changed her name when she
got married? Playing the lottery never looked so good. And then
Bea called us to supper.

———

We had just returned to the office, after a wonderful meal of
grilled goat chops with garlic, oregano, and lemon; brown rice;
buttered peas with pearl onions, dill, and watercress; and a lettuce
salad, when the phone rang. I answered.

"Wright Investigations."

"Is this Mr. Wright?"

"It is."

"This is LaQueesha Washington. You left a message on my phone. How can I help you?"

"We're conducting an investigation and as I said in the message, Jawanda Clark told us you might have some information that would be of help. Would it be possible for you to come to our place and talk about it?" I gave her the address.

"Well, you see Mr. Wright, I have to put Jimmy to bed soon. He's my boy."

"Would it be okay if I came to your place?"

"Uh, sure. That would be fine. You'll be here soon? You don't live far."

"I'm leaving now, if that's okay."

"That's fine."

I got the address from her and hung up the phone.

"That was LaQueesha Washington. You ladies want to come along?"

Tina said no. Bea said yes. And, of course, Bea volunteered to drive. In a minute we were out the door and in fifteen we were at LaQueesha's place.

Her home was a typical South Minneapolis bungalow. When we rang the doorbell she answered the door, I showed her my credentials and introduced Bea and myself. She invited us in.

"Can I get you something?" she asked.

We told her we were fine.

"So what do you want to know?"

"I understand, Ms. Washington, you overheard part of a conversation between Prisca Thoraldson and somebody. What did you exactly hear?"

"Well, you see, she was outside and I was outside, you know in the parking lot. I needed some fresh air for a minute. I don't know why Prisca was outside. She was on her cell and I don't think she realized I was there. She was saying something about she had it and she wouldn't be able to meet until the day after tomorrow. Then she got all agitated and raised her voice. Whoever she was talking to must've calmed her down because she became a lot quieter. The whole thing sounded suspicious and I told Jawanda about it. But the more I thought about it the more I realized it could be nothing. She might've been talking about hand towels for all I know."

"That's certainly possible. Is that it?"

"It is. I'm sorry. Wish I had more."

"No need to be sorry, Ms. Washington. Detective work is nothing more than gathering a bunch of little pieces and then seeing if they can be put together to form a big picture. You gave us some little pieces. They might be important and they might not. Won't know until we see if and where they fit."

We thanked her and left.

In the car on the way home, Bea said what I was thinking. "That was a waste, Harry. Prisca could've been talking to anybody about anything."

"Very true, Babe. Then again, it might be just what we need. In all likelihood, though, this was a wild goose chase."

———

At quarter to nine Wikstrom was in the oversized oxblood wingback, with a vodka seven in her hand. Ross Felder was on one end of the chesterfield, a glass of Petite Syrah in his hand, and Bea was on the other end, with a hot chocolate.

Tina and Wikstrom were sizing each other up, Felder was checking out the ceiling, Bea was tatting, and I was taking it all in. Pen poised above paper, just waiting for a chance to use my shorthand. Finally Wikstrom spoke.

"I'm not the one leaking information and neither is Ross."

"Who is?" Tina asked.

"I don't know."

"Who's your best guess?"

"I'm not convinced there is a spy. Alex seems to think so.

Personally? I think it's a ploy to get rid of Prisca. You heard about the Alex and Prisca brouhaha?"

"I did."

"Ever since, Alex has been lobbying to get rid of Prisca."

"So you don't think there's a spy."

"No. Alex has all this evidence," she made quote marks in the air when she said the word *evidence*, "she says indicates someone's leaking information. However, first off," she took a sip of her drink, "there isn't that much evidence. And, second, it could all be coincidence. I think Mad threw two hundred thousand down the toilet hiring you."

"You weren't in favor."

"No, I wasn't. About the only thing Alex and I have been agreed on."

Tina took a sip of wine. "So you don't think the dissension with Alex Brewer has driven anyone to sell out the campaign."

"No."

"What about you, Mr. Felder?"

Ross came back to planet earth. "Uh, no, I don't. There are a few of us who think Alex should go. That she's no longer right for the campaign. Aside from that, everyone is one hundred percent behind Mad. None of us would do anything to endanger the campaign."

Tina sat back in her chair and closed her eyes.

Bea said, "A lot of people are telling us Prisca Thoraldson would endanger the campaign to get back at Alex Brewer."

Wikstrom looked at Bea. "That's because she's about as pleasant to work with as dragging your hand down a rose stem. She's honey to the donors and acid to everyone else."

Tina sat up. "Why?"

"How the hell would I know? Maybe she has permanent PMS."

That one got a smile out of Tina.

"Ms. Wikstrom, thank you for your insights. You, too, Mr. Felder. Please drive home safely."

Wikstrom was surprised. "We're done?"

"Unless you have more information."

Felder downed his wine. "C'mon, Susan. We have a long day tomorrow."

I saw Wikstrom and Felder to the door, wished them good-night, and returned to the Inner Sanctum.

"Were they helpful?" I asked.

Tina stood. "They were helpful. Goodnight, you two."

She left and Bea and I relocated to the living room.

"Harry, my love?"

"Yes, Babe?"

"What if Susan is right?"

"Then Alex is going to end up hearing what she doesn't want to hear."

"I wouldn't want to be around when that happens."

"While it's possible, I don't think it's probable."

"What do you mean?"

"I'm just saying, Babe, I've been doing this long enough to trust my gut and my gut's telling me there's something going on. Those two are just in denial."

12

LUCKY BREAK

Friday. September 26th

WE WERE IN THE OFFICE BY NINE. PRUDY WAS CURLED UP ON TINA'S desk. Manly and Buddy were chasing each other up and down stairs and hallways. Isis was probably under a blanket somewhere. The humans were sitting at their respective desks and even though the sky was cloudy, a light breeze and a temp in the low sixties called for open windows. Especially when Tina fired up a cigar.

The Great Detective had decided last night to send Gwen Poisson, an excellent freelance operative and computer hacker she frequently uses when we need extra arms and legs, to see what she could get from Fishman. A note taped to my door up on the third floor asked me to call her. Tina having put it there before she went to bed. Given the hour, I'd texted Gwen instead of calling and was surprised when she texted right back saying she'd be on it first thing this morning.

Today, I was working the Ted Horstman angle and spent the morning gleaning what I could about him from the web, trying to add to the information I'd gotten previously, both on the web and in person.

Along about noon, Gwen called in to say she'd been able to hack Fishman's smartphone using her Universal Forensic Extraction Device and was going over the data to see what might be of use.

Having gleaned what I could from online data, I decided to get my hands dirty and see what I could glean out in the real world. I told the ladies I'd see them when I'd see them and left the comforts of home for the unknown of working out in the field. My first stop, though, was at my favorite White Castle in northeast Minneapolis and once I had lunch safely stowed away, I went in search of Ted Horstman.

I decided to start at his company and drove out to Plymouth, in my Focus this time, and searched the parking lot for his orange BMW. No luck. Perhaps he was at lunch. If that was the case, he could be anywhere. I decided to try the Horstman home down in Minnetonka.

There were no cars in the driveway. I parked on the street and walked up the drive to the front door. Curtains were pulled across the windows, preventing me from looking in. I rang the doorbell and waited. No answer. I rang again. No answer that time either. No one home. Or they weren't answering the door. I walked back down the drive to my car and got in.

I could go home and try again tomorrow morning. I could go to his company and wait. Or I could sit right where I was and wait. Conducting surveillance in a neighborhood is always tricky. People notice things and will too often call the cops, which too often blows your cover or forces you to break off the surveillance when the cop tells you to move along. I decided to drive out to the company offices and see if I could pick him up there.

Back out to the blah beige office building which was home to the headquarters of Clean Sweep, Inc. I drove through the parking lot and spotted the BMW. I found a parking space two rows back and four cars down. The front of my car faced away from his. I adjusted the rearview mirrors so I could see his car and waited to see if I could see him.

Two hours and forty-seven minutes later he left the building and got into his Beemer. I started the Focus and when he was rolling I backed out of my spot, readjusted my mirrors, and followed. What became apparent very quickly was wherever he was going it wasn't home. He drove out Highway 55 and then went north on I-494. I followed and when he turned east onto I-694 I was right there with him about four car lengths behind. He exited onto Boone Avenue going north, turned onto Northland Drive, and drove into the parking lot of the Marriott hotel. I let him park and picked a spot two rows behind him. He sat in the car for a few minutes and then got out and headed for the main entrance. I snapped several photos.

What to do? If I followed him into the hotel, I ran the risk of him seeing me. My guess was he was there to meet someone. I decided to sit tight and observe the main entrance with my binoculars. Luck was on my side. I only had to wait twenty-two minutes before I saw Prisca Thoraldson walk into the hotel. I took a few pictures of her as well.

"Harry, my man," I said to my faithful car, "I think you found the mole and the mole's information source. In addition, it looks as though you uncovered a little bit of adultery going on as well."

I sat and watched the entrance. Nearly two hours later, first Ted emerged, followed ten minutes later by Prisca. And I got them nicely recorded on the camera's chip.

"You've earned your pay for today, old boy." I had to admit I was very pleased with myself. "Maybe LaQueesha's snippet of overheard conversation has more merit to it than we gave it credit for."

I watched them drive away and, after they were gone, put the car in drive and pointed the nose towards that wonderful place I call home.

———

The traffic on the freeway was abysmal. Once I was across the river, I got off the parking lot and took the side streets to West Franklin. I pulled into the drive at a quarter to six, just in time for supper.

Buddy greeted me when I walked in the door, followed by Bea. Tina was in the music room playing something by Arthur Foote.

"Supper's ready, Sweetie Pie. Want to let Tina know?"

"Sure, Babe."

I went to the music room. Tina saw me standing in the doorway and stopped playing.

"Is supper ready?"

"It is."

She stood, walked to me, gave me a hug, and together we walked into the dining room.

When Bea saw us, she started smiling. "It's so good to have you back."

Tina gave Bea a hug and we sat down to eat the wonderful Provençal Rainbow Soup, with zucchini, onion, garlic, olives, tomatoes, and anchovies, plus the sausage-stuffed acorn squash. The California Chenin Blanc was a nice addition.

Since talking shop is *verboten* at the table, I just mentioned we needed to gather in the office afterward. Tina nodded and then started talking about the young rising stars among the new generation of Chinese musicians. When supper was over, Tina actually helped us clear the table and put the dishes in the dishwasher. We then took our tea and the Spotted Dick Bea had made to the office. Tina and I settled in at our desks and Bea took over a corner of the chesterfield.

I took a bite of the steamed pudding. "Hey, Babe, this is great!"

Tina concurred. "It tastes like more."

Bea was beaming. "Thanks, guys!"

With spoon poised in mid-air, Tina said, "What do you have for us, Harry?", and then let it and the pudding continue on to her mouth.

I held up the camera. "In here are pictures of Ted Horstman and Prisca Thoraldson meeting at the Marriott in Brooklyn Park, off 694."

Tina took a sip of tea. "Interesting. Puts LaQueesha's information into a whole new light. We must certainly ask the question is Ted Horstman in league with Prisca Thoraldson? If so, is she simply passing him information or is he passing something back in return?"

"My money is on information being exchanged for sex," I said.

"That's awful," Bea said. Adultery is a touchy subject for my honey since her late hife, Alicia, had cheated on her prior to Alicia's murder.

"It is," Tina concurred. She has her own issues, such as Cal throwing her over for his blond bombshell partner.

Personally, I think adultery is pretty normal. People like sex. People like variety. Everyone is unfaithful, if only in their imagination. Except me, of course. And, yes, my tongue is in my cheek. I love Bea and have no intention to cheat on her, but the imagination is an unruly beast and at times difficult to control. However, I wasn't going to give those two an opportunity to turn me into a punching bag. No sirree Bob.

Instead, I asked, "What are we going to do with this info?"

"Good question, Harry." Tina fished a cigar out of the humidor. "Right now the pictures are pretty much worthless unless we can get corroborating evidence. LaQueesha didn't give us enough. Her bit does help direct the path." She lit the panetela and sent a cloud of smoke to the ceiling. "Maybe we can do our own sting operation."

"How so?" I asked.

"We plant false information that is discussed in the morning meeting and then follow Mr. Horstman and Prisca and see who they meet up with, if they meet up with anybody, and follow that person back to Aagard's headquarters."

"And then we'll know," Bea said.

"And then we'll know who's leaking information to Aagard's

campaign," Tina confirmed. "We'll also want to make sure the information is something on which Aagard will act. That will be double confirmation."

"Any idea what fake piece of info will do the trick?" I asked.

"Not yet," Tina replied. "We can discuss that with the Congresswoman. In the meantime, since we haven't finished talking to everyone on the campaign, I think we need to talk to the other staffers just in case Horstman and Thoraldson are scratching a totally different itch. One unrelated to the passing on of campaign secrets."

"That still leaves us with Fishman and the sugar baby issue."

Tina puffed on her cigar. "It does, Harry. We'll see if Gwen comes up with anything."

As if on cue, the phone rang. I answered, "Wright Investigations."

"Hi, Harry. Gwen."

"Hi, Gwen. I'm putting you on speaker."

"Hi, Tina."

"Hello, Gwen. Bea is with us."

"Hi, Bea. How are you?"

"I'm good, Gwen. Thanks."

"Great. Tina, I just finished going over the info on Fishman's phone. Nothing."

"Nothing?"

"Nothing pertaining to the case. I'm wondering if he has a different phone he uses for his blackmailing operations."

"Certainly possible."

"You want me to keep on him?"

"For now. See if anything comes up."

"Will do. Ciao."

"Bye, Gwen."

The call ended, I hung up the phone. Tina was leaning back in her chair, cigar jutting out of her mouth, hands behind her head. She sat that way for some time and then sat up.

"Harry, how did Fishman get the sugar baby information?"

"I don't know. Probably in the course of digging up dirt on Horstman."

"Correct. Who does the digging?"

"Staffers. But for something that remote, I'd say he probably hired a detective."

"I'd say you are correct. See if you can find out who."

"Will do."

"With Gwen checking out Fishman, I want you to continue observing Ted Horstman. Let's see if there is a pattern to what he does. I'll see if I can come up with something to use in the sting operation."

With business taken care of, we left the office and went to the living room. We decided to watch a movie. Bea made popcorn and I got out pop for us to have with the popcorn. A root beer for Bea, an orange cream for Tina, and a birch beer for myself. Bea had never seen *Sunset Boulevard*, so we decided to watch that one.

The time was a little after eleven when we finished the movie and decided to call it a night. That's when my cell phone started ringing. I took it out of my pocket and looked at it. Gwen was calling.

"Hey Gwen, what's up?"

"Harry, I'm in Fishman's house and he's dead. Shot in the chest. What does Tina want me to do?"

I turned to the Boss. "It's Gwen. Fishman's been murdered. She wants instructions."

Tina took the phone from me. "Gwen, see if you can find the secret cell phone. If you do, strip it of info. See if you can find anything about Horstman being a sugar baby and take it. Then call the police." She paused a moment and then said, "Bye."

She handed me back my phone. I said, "Looks like the Congresswoman got a lucky break."

"Maybe, Harry. Maybe."

13

MACHINATIONS

Saturday. September 27th

THE TIME WAS HALF-PAST NINE IN THE MORNING AND THE DOORBELL rang. Tina and I were at our desks and hard at work. Bea was out grocery shopping.

Tina was ruminating on the information Gwen had given us last night. Her first call at eleven telling us Fishman was dead and her subsequent call an hour and a half later to let us know she hadn't been able to find either the secret cell phone or information on Madelyn's adventures as a sugar baby. Gwen did find a wall safe and a floor safe, but no combinations for either one. When she was done with her search, she made an anonymous call to the police to report Fishman's death.

I was phoning and emailing our local coterie of private detectives trying to find one who'd admit he or she did work for the now dead Fishman and I wasn't having any luck. His death hadn't made the morning paper, but did get a mention on the radio.

At the sound of the doorbell, I went to the door, looked through the peephole, and returned to the office.

"I think you are probably going to want to relocate. A certain

Minneapolis police lieutenant connected with the Homicide division is on our doorstep."

Tina glared at me.

"Hey! Don't shoot the messenger."

"Sorry." She stood and left the office.

I went back out to the door and opened it. "Good morning, Cal."

"Hi, Harry. I suppose—"

I shook my head.

"I thought so. You know anything about the Fishman murder?"

"And why would we know anything about that?"

"The rumor mill has it you're working for Madelyn Horstman and he was her primary opponent."

"Heard mention on the radio this morning."

"I see. That's all?"

"I'm afraid so. How are you involved?"

"I'm not. Didn't happen in the city. A deputy buddy of mine asked."

"I see. Well, sorry I can't help you."

"The flowers…?"

I shook my head. I didn't have the heart to tell him they went in the garbage disposal.

"Yeah. Well, uh, I'd best be going. Nice seeing you, Harry. Tell Bea I said 'hi', will you?"

"Same here, Cal, and I'll greet Bea for you."

He gave me a nod, turned around, and set off down the walk. That was one beaten down man. I returned to the office and sat at my desk. I have to confess, that was odd. His coming here like that. Damn odd, in fact. Then again, people are damn odd. So why am I surprised? I went back to work and in a while Tina returned.

She sat at her desk. "What did he want?"

"Wanted to know if we knew anything about the Fishman murder."

"Are you serious?"

"I am."

"It didn't even happen in his jurisdiction."

"He admitted as much."

She shook her head. "Wanted to see me. That's what he really wanted."

"Possibly. He did ask me to greet Bea for him. Didn't mention you."

She gave me a look and then turned her eyes to something on her desk.

I went back to phone calls and emails.

Along about eleven, Tina broke her silence.

"This is where we are at. Fishman's dead and most likely so is the sugar baby issue. No way to know for sure, because he could have had a partner. Probably not, but it is possible. I think it unlikely Tricia Long, if that is still her name, will use the information against Madelyn Horstman. Did you get anywhere on the private eye check?"

"Nope. If someone local did the work for Fishman, that someone is either not saying or I haven't run across him or her yet."

"Drop it for now."

"Glad to."

"We have evidence Ted Horstman and Prisca Thoraldson are meeting. We don't know why, but are assuming it's for sex and the passing on of information.

"Thus far we've talked with Alex Brewer, the Horstmans, Damon Rossiter, Vi Nguyen, Jawanda Clark, Prisca Thoraldson, Susan Wikstrom, and Ross Felder. The conclusion being no one likes Alex, people are willing to point the finger at Prisca, and everyone, save for Brewer and Mad Horstman, thinks Brewer is the problem.

"In addition to those connected with Horstman's campaign, we've talked to Jim Oberman on Aagard's campaign and may arrange to swap money for information. We have yet to talk with

Chelsea Lindstrom, Brewer's assistant, and Darius Littlewood of the main staff, as well as the three regular volunteers Brewer doesn't like. I think that sums up where we are at this moment."

"Seems like you've hit all the points, Sis. Who do we tackle first?"

"For now, I think we'll focus on Ted and Prisca and talk to Lindstrom and Littlewood."

"Sounds good to me. And if I might add, it's good to have you back. I don't like being the boss."

"Why thank you, Harry. I'm glad to be back. I like my home and, as much as I complain, I like the work."

Well, folks, you heard it here first. She really does like the work.

"You're welcome, Sis. I missed you. Bea and I both did. Don't do that again, unless you take us with you."

She laughed. "Okay. Now I know you're just angling for a vacation."

"Doggone it. I'm just too transparent."

"I won't, Big Brother. I'm done running away. Doing so solves nothing."

The time was closing in on noon. I decided to make lunch and got up from my desk. The phone rang. I answered, "Wright Investigations."

The voice on the other end was muffled. "Meet me in the parking lot off Godfrey Parkway just east of Minnehaha Avenue. Tonight at eleven. I'll be in a blue Toyota Avalon. Code is 'What is an elephant?'. I'll answer, 'The way to victory.' Be there. Eleven." Then I was left with a dial tone.

"You look puzzled, Harry. What is it?"

I told her what the voice said to me.

"Hm. Mysterious. I guess I know where we'll be at eleven."

"You're coming along?"

"Sure. Sounds like something from my days in the Company."

"Glad to have you along. If we use the Flex or my car, Bea can join us."

Tina thought a moment. "Okay. We'll make it a threesome."

With that settled, I made my way to the kitchen to work on lunch and noticed Bea had pulled in the driveway. In a moment, she was walking in the backdoor.

"Hi, Harry!"

"Hey, Babe. I'll get the groceries."

"I got lunch for us."

"You did?"

"Uh-huh. Roast chicken, potato salad, and coleslaw."

"I guess that will save me some work."

Bea and I hauled in the grocery bags, put the food away, and then set out the lunch grub. She had a beer. Tina and I, French Colombard.

To pass the afternoon, Tina decided to go out to the campaign headquarters and Bea and I went out to the Horstman residence. There was no evidence anyone was home. A knock on the door revealed the children were home and a neighbor girl was babysitting. I asked when she thought the Horstmans would be home. She didn't know. Mad was speaking at a luncheon and then a dinner. Ted was at the office.

Bea asked, "Why would he be at work on a Saturday?"

The girl replied, "Major cleaning is done on the weekends when the businesses are closed."

Made sense to me. We thanked her and left.

"Now where are we going, Harry?"

"Well, Sugar Plum, I think we'll go to his office by way of the hotel.

"Oh, I get it. He might not be working at all."

"Right."

Bea giggled.

"What's so funny?"

"I just got thinking maybe he was giving a personal carpet cleaning demo."

"God, Bea. Sometimes you have the dirtiest mind."

She laughed. "Yeah, but you never seem to mind."

"You have me there."

"Oh, Harry. I'm so madly in love with you. Why do you love me?"

"There's really no explanation for love. I just do. Things I like about you are your genuineness, simplicity, honesty, and openness. Nothing fake about you. And to quote the song, 'I love how you love me'."

"I wish Tina and Cal would get over their issues."

"Well, I don't see that happening. In fact, I think it's over between them."

"That's sad. Very sad."

"It is."

We arrived at the hotel. I drove through the parking lot, but didn't see Ted's car anywhere. I decided to park and wait a bit. The time was two-ish. The afternoon was still young. But when no one showed up by three, I drove over to Ted's office. And there was his car. I parked and we waited.

Within fifteen minutes, Prisca Thoraldson exited the building. I photographed her all the way from door to car and even managed to snap a pic of her license plate.

"So much for him checking up on his cleaning crews," Bea said.

"As you pointed out, Babe, he was giving a customer personal attention."

"God, Harry, I'm so horny. Do you think…?"

Of course I think and two minds are better than one. We figured out a way to solve little Bea's problem and then drove on home where, before supper, we engaged in further problem solving. Which was also why our evening meal was pizza from Jakeeno's and a tossed salad of various greens, cucumber, radish, celery, grape tomatoes, and shredded beets.

Tina was back by suppertime and because of her rule about where and when we talk shop, our supper conversation was about Ralph Vaughan Williams's proficiency as a composer of piano music. The conclusion being he was more than adequate.

When supper was over, we retired with tea and cookies to the office.

"So what was going on over at campaign central?" I asked.

Tina set down her tea cup. "Brewer was quietly jubilant. She and the Congresswoman are very confident the sugar baby threat is dead."

"That's just sick!" Bea exclaimed. "The man was killed!"

"From their point of view, a major threat to the campaign is gone," Tina replied. "Of course, Brewer was sorry that Fishman died — but not too sorry."

"That's just awful," Bea said. "The man was murdered."

"Were you sorry when your hife was murdered?"

"Tina, that's not fair. Alicia was really mean and abusive."

"Fishman was mean and a blackmailer, Bea."

I could tell my cupcake was not convinced. She didn't continue the discussion. I asked, "Do we have an idea for a sting operation?"

"Not yet. Brewer didn't like my idea."

"Which was?" I asked.

"To leak how Horstman was going to vote on a bill, or that she was authoring a piece of legislation on a controversial issue."

"What did Brewer want to do?"

"Didn't have an idea."

"Probably opposed to yours because she didn't come up with it."

"Could be. I was hoping to talk to Lindstrom, but she was out with Wikstrom and Felder on a literature drop. I spoke a little bit with Darius Littlewood. He didn't have much to say. Just avoids Brewer and does his job which is making sure all of their equipment works and that the website is updated. He doesn't impress me as a mole."

"Good," I said. "That's one we can take off the list."

"You tell Bea about the adventure we're going to have tonight?"

"Harry told me." By her tone of voice I could tell my little sugar plum was still peeved.

If Tina noticed, she ignored it. "Good. We should probably be there early to look things over."

"Sounds like a plan," I replied.

Bea said nothing. She was still peeved.

———

We pulled into the parking lot at twenty to eleven. The lot is in two sections and was deserted except for five cars, none of which were a blue Toyota Avalon. I was driving my Focus. Tina was in the front passenger seat and Bea was in back.

"Harry, drive out and re-enter," Tina said.

I drove out the exit, circled back around to the entrance, and drove back in. The same five cars were in the lot. Two in the one section and three in the other. I drove out and stopped along the curb of the street. The entrance was not visible from where we were parked. We waited for ten minutes and then Tina gave me the go ahead to re-enter the lot. The time was five before eleven.

I drove slowly through the one section and made the turn to go down the remaining section when I spotted the blue Toyota Avalon. The car was parked head in. The lights were off and the driver's side was away from us. I stopped the Focus in the driving lane and put it in park.

"Bea, wait here," Tina said.

Tina and I got out at the same time and walked to the Toyota. She waited by the right rear quarter panel and I walked around to the driver's side. That's when I saw the shattered driver's window and a very dead Damon Rossiter.

14

SPIES AND COUNTER-SPIES

Sunday. September 28th

WE WERE BACK HOME IN TIME FOR BREAKFAST. TINA, HOWEVER, WAS IN no mood for eating or anything else and the reason was Cal Swenson. She had to answer his questions, because he insisted on questioning her alone. Rather nasty on his part, although on one level I can't blame him. He saw an opportunity to talk to Tina and he took it.

On the drive home all Bea or I could get out of her was, "That man!"

At the breakfast table, with a plate of eggs, bacon, and toast getting cold, she blurted out, "The nerve. The goddamn nerve."

In the office, I finally got her to be a bit more informative.

"He actually threatened to take me downtown."

I said, "Okay. Why?"

"Because I wasn't going to tell him one goddamn thing. I told him I wanted to talk to another officer. He said his partner was busy and I'd have to talk to him. And he actually called me 'Tina'."

"That is your name," I said.

She glowered at me. "I told him I was 'Miss Wright' to him."

"Did you answer his questions?"

"I did."

"I see you're still alive."

"Shit. My own brother."

She stood and marched out of the office. A little while later I went to look for her and couldn't find her. Bea told me she was in her room. I thought on that a moment, returned to the office, built a fire in the fireplace, stretched out on the couch, and took a nap. After all, we didn't get much sleep during the night.

————

Bea woke me for lunch. She'd made us Dagwood sandwiches. When she'd checked on Tina, the Great Detective had put a "Do Not Disturb" sign on her door. So it was just my honey and I lunching together.

With my sandwich safely stowed away, I drove out to Horstman Campaign Central. I wanted to see what state of disarray things were in and I wasn't disappointed. The place was a zoo. News of Rossiter's murder had spread like wild fire. Over half the volunteers didn't show up or left as soon as they found out.

The campaign committee was in a closed door meeting. Brewer's assistant, Chelsea Lindstrom, was doing her best to keep the volunteers who'd remained busy working on stuffing envelopes. They, however, seemed more interested in gossiping.

I wandered around, listening to snippets of conversation, all was idle speculation. Finally, I decided to have a talk with Chelsea to see if I could find out anything. She was at her desk, in a little cubicle, stuffing envelopes.

"How can I help you? You're one of the consultants, aren't you?"

I admitted I was. I asked, "What's going to happen now that Damon's gone?"

"That's what they're meeting about now. Awful. Just awful. He was such a nice guy. You meet him?"

"I did and, yes, he seemed like a nice guy."

"He was really behind Mad."

Hm. Now that was interesting. If we ran with my guess, it was that he was a spy for Aagard. And if he was, then he must have been a hell of a good actor. As well as being nice.

"I don't know, Chelsea, if you know, or if you can tell me if you do, I'm wondering if Mad has a spy working for her in Aagard's campaign?"

"Oh, she'd never do that. She's very ethical and above board."

"How about Alex?"

There Chelsea faltered. She hesitated far too long. In the end, she did say, "Alex might."

"Might or does?"

"Uh, well," she glanced at my name tag, "Harry, I don't know for sure—"

"C'mon Chelsea, this is important. You folks have someone leaking information to Aagard. I need to know if Alex has an operative in the enemy's camp. Maybe the two are working together."

"Honest, Harry, I don't know. She might. That would be Alex's style."

"Okay. I'll run with that."

"Please don't say anything."

"Don't worry. I won't. How do you get on with Alex?"

"All right."

"How long have you worked here?"

"I just came on board last year."

"If Mad wins, will you be going to Washington?"

"I think so. Alex says I'll be the Deputy Chief of Staff. That's an important job and it pays pretty good, too."

"You must get on more than 'all right' with Alex if she's going to make you the deputy chief."

Chelsea looked at me. I could see something in her eyes. Was it animosity? Fear? I wasn't sure.

"We get along with each other just fine. I do what I'm told and do it well."

"Who do you think is the mole? The one leaking the information?"

"I think it's Prisca. She hates Alex and I think she's trying to ruin the campaign to ruin Alex."

"You think she's working alone?"

That one stumped her. She took a while to answer. "Probably. There are others who don't like Alex. Susan Wikstrom is one of them. She might be working with Prisca. But then she is the District Director when in Washington, so I don't think she'd want to sink the campaign."

"I guess that makes sense. What does Prisca do in Washington?"

"She's the Projects and Grants Coordinator."

"So why would she want to sink the campaign?"

"I don't know. Maybe she hates Alex more than she likes the job."

"Makes sense, I guess. Thanks for the chat. I'll let you get back to work."

I left her cube and wandered around a bit. Wikstrom was probably in the meeting. Where might Felder be? I poked my head back into Chelsea's office.

"Say, do you happen to know where Ross Felder is?"

"Not off hand. He might be coordinating a literature drop. Weekends are good for that. We get more volunteers on the weekend."

"Sure. Makes sense. Thanks again, Chelsea."

I decided I'd had enough for one day. I walked out, said goodbye to Opal, and continued on to my car.

Sunday, late afternoon, and the freeway was crowded. Doesn't anyone stay home these days? I putzed along 494 until I got to 100 and then putzed along 100 until I got to West 50th Street. There, I ditched the freeway and took the local roads.

When I arrived at the little mansion I call home, sweet home, Bea was making supper and Tina was in the music room playing Liszt's piano transcription of Beethoven's Ninth Symphony. I kissed Bea, copped a couple radishes, and went to the office.

I stoked up the fire, sat on the couch, and watched the flames. One will get you fifty, Rossiter was sending information back to Aagard's campaign and probably spreading false info at the same time to Horstman's. Yet, many a finger was pointed at Prisca. Were all those fingers wrong? Was she simply screwing her candidate's husband? Or was she in fact a traitor and those pointing fingers justified?

And what about Ted Horstman? Was he also a traitor? Or was he simply screwing one of his wife's staffers? One will get you fifty the latter's true. As to the former, well, now, I was no longer sure.

Once again, Wikstrom's name came up as someone who wasn't an Alex fan. We might have to talk to her and Felder again. There was obviously some distrust there. My conversation with Chelsea left me with the nagging suspicion she was one of Alex's playthings and therefore wasn't going to upset a good thing.

The question did beg to be asked, were the murders of Fishman and Rossiter connected? My gut said yes. But for the life of me I didn't see an obvious connection.

Bea announced supper was ready and I walked with her to the dining room. Tina joined us for the Shepherd's Pie my little pooky had prepared. Bea drank water, Tina and I had a Minnesota Frontenac. The dinner conversation was a discussion on the merits of wine produced from hybrid grapes versus the so-called "noble" varieties. I think Tina summed it up when she said, "Good wine is good wine. No matter what the grape." Very true. Especially considering there's an awful lot of insipid, nondescript Cabernet out there.

After supper, we retired to the office so I could report on my trip to the campaign headquarters. I relayed what I'd observed and learned and when I was done Tina lit a cigar and leaned back in her chair. She pushed out her lips and just sat there. Sixty-seven seconds passed. The lips returned to normal, she took a puff on her cigar, and sat up.

"See if Ted Horstman and Prisca Thoraldson will agree to come here for a chat."

"Do you want them together or separately?"

"Doesn't matter, Harry, and see if David Nagasawa's available. I want him to plant through the wall listening devices in Ted Horstman's office, his home, and at Thoraldson's residence. I want you to put a bug in Thoraldson's office at the campaign headquarters. Oh, if David can bug their cars, that would be very satisfactory."

Bea asked, "Isn't that illegal?"

Tina replied, "We aren't going to court on this, so the legality is, for me, irrelevant. I'm trying to get information. Are those two simply screwing, or are they also screwing the Congresswoman?"

Bea persisted, "But aren't you violating their rights?"

"Technically, yes. So they can sue me. If David's good, and he is, the odds are we won't get caught."

Tina's right. David's good. Very good. The best freelancer south of the North Pole. And Gwen, who was looking into Fishman, is right behind him.

"Do you want to talk to Wikstrom and Felder again?"

"Yes, I would like to, but I don't think doing so will get us anywhere."

I leaned back in my chair, crossed my legs, and put my hands behind my head. "I know this is a sore spot, but did Cal give you any details?"

"Actually, he did. I think he was, in his own way, trying to be nice to me. He said he thought the caliber was small. Maybe a twenty-five. I'd already come to that conclusion. He also said he'd share the results of the autopsy report."

"That's very nice of him," I said.

"He also suggested we work together on the case."

Bea's face lit up like a searchlight. "Really? Oh, wow!"

"I told him there was no way in hell of that happening. He said he understood and hoped I'd change my mind. I told him I doubted that would happen. Better chance of snow falling in the Amazon."

Bea's face looked like an imploding building. She likes Cal a lot. I don't think she'd throw me over for him. It's not that kind of like. What she wants is for him and Tina to get together, so he can live here in Tina's little mansion with us. From the sounds of it, that ain't happening anytime in the near, or maybe even distant, future. Yep, I think they've come to the end of the road.

Bea blurted out, "But Tina, you love him."

"Correction, Bea. I think *loved* is the correct form of the verb."

Bea jumped up from the chesterfield and ran from the room.

Tina looked at me.

"She likes Cal a lot. So do I, for that matter."

"Harry, how can you say that after what he did to me?"

"I'm not excusing his actions. Yes, he did a big bad. But people do make mistakes. Sometimes big, huge, ugly, messy ones. Cal made a doozy and he admits it. For what it's worth, I think he wishes he could turn back the clock and erase that mistake."

"What's done is done. He is *persona non grata* here."

"Whatever you say. It's your house." I stood. "I'm going to check on Bea."

I found my sweet pea in our bedroom. She was lying on the bed and had been crying. The tears were gone now. Her face, though, was tear-stained. I lay next to her and held her. Things are going to be different around here without Cal. I suppose we'll get used to it. Life is nothing but change. If you don't get used to the constant stream of changes, you're going to have no end of problems.

15

INTERROGATIONS

Monday. September 29th

BREAKFAST WAS MORE OR LESS OUR NORMAL ROUTINE. TEA, TOAST, soft-boiled eggs, bacon, and a fruit salad were on the table.

Tina's nose was in her iPad. Bea and I were sharing the newspaper. Buddy was under Bea's chair, Manly waiting in the wings to pounce on him. Isis and Prudy were over by Tina.

That the household was still out of kilter due to a certain homicide detective talking to a certain private detective was evident in that Tina said not one word about newsprint or germs from the paper getting on our hands.

In fact, she said not a single word before or during breakfast. When we said good morning to her, she merely nodded her head at us. When she'd drunk her second cup of tea and eaten her slice of toast, she stood, said "office", and left. One word. I think that is a new record.

"Babe, you mind cleaning up? I need to make sure the ship of state isn't heading for the reef."

"Sure, Harry, my love."

I kissed her and went to the office. Tina was at her desk. I sat at mine. I made phone calls and with a bit of cajoling and arm twisting got both Ted and Prisca to agree to pay us a visit as soon as possible today.

On the off chance I might succeed, I called both Susan Wikstrom and Ross Felder to see if they could stop by today. Wikstrom was no go. She said she was too busy. If we wanted to talk to her, then make an appointment to meet at the headquarters. So I did for tomorrow morning. Felder was also too busy and didn't even give me the option of an appointment.

David was on a job. However, he thought he could squeeze us in. When I told him what Tina wanted, he said to give him a few days to get it all done.

My part mostly accomplished, I still had to bug Prisca's office, I turned my attention to the Great Detective. She was reading a book, at least I assumed it was a book, on her iPad.

"Do you know how you're going to approach Ted and Prisca?"

She didn't bother looking up. "Yes."

"Mind sharing so I can come in out of the cold."

That got her to look up. "What is it you want, Harry?"

"You're not angry with me, are you?"

She redirected her attention back to her iPad. "No."

"If you don't care about Cal, why are you letting him affect you?"

She set the iPad down and glared at me. "What is with you two? Cal's not the only man on the planet."

"No, he's not. But he is one man who loves you and is willing to admit he made a huge mistake."

"I'm done with him."

"Then why are you acting as though you still care?"

"Oh, for God's sake." She stood and marched out of the office.

I shook my head and called Horstman campaign headquarters, got Opal the receptionist, and asked her if Prisca Thoraldson was in.

"Yes, she is, Mr. Wright. Should I put you through to her?"

"No. That's okay. What's her schedule like this week?"

Opal outlined when Prisca was scheduled to be out of the

office. I took notes, thanked her, and hung up the phone. Tomorrow looked good for me to step around and do the bug planting. I have a nifty little device I can activate with my cell phone. I just needed a good place to hide it.

Bea was at her desk in the outer office. I told her I was going to make lunch and that sometime today Ted Horstman and Prisca Thoraldson would be showing up.

"I'll let you know when they're here, my darling," she said and blew a kiss at me.

"Thanks, Cupcake. Know where Tina is?"

"No, I don't."

I kissed her and went to the kitchen. Today, for lunch, I decided to make cabbage roll casserole. A delicious way to get all the advantages of the roll and not have to do any rolling. Music is always a nice accompaniment to preparing a meal. I turned on the iPod and listened to Wagner overtures. *Rienzi, Die Meistersinger, Flying Dutchman, Tannhauser*. I was two minutes into the Prelude to Act I of *Lohengrin* when Bea told me Ted was going to arrive around one-thirty and Prisca would be knocking at our door around four. The clock on the stove told me lunch was going to be a little tight. I increased the oven temp a bit and hoped for the best.

Things turned out just fine. Today's topic of discussion was the music of Sir Granville Bantock, Tina holding forth on the thought Hollywood should have snapped him up for movie scores. If they had done so, the movies of the '30s would have had some truly superb music. As it was, I think they did alright. Nevertheless, Tina had a point.

The Boss and I got to the office with seven minutes to spare, for our guest was early. I let him in, introduced him to Miss Wright, and steered him towards the oversized oxblood wingback.

Horstman began the discussion. "Well, Miss Wright, what is it I can help you with?"

"How well do you know Prisca Thoraldson?"

He smiled. "How well do you think I know her?"

"I think you are intimately acquainted with her."

"Is that so?"

"It is."

"And what if I said, 'prove it'?"

"I'd say I'm well on my way to do so."

He was quiet for a few moments before he said, "What's the point?"

"I'm trying to find the mole in your wife's campaign and I think *the* mole is actually *two* moles: you and Miss Thoraldson. She gets the information and you pass it on to Aagard's campaign."

"And why on earth would I want to do that?"

"So your wife can be here in Minnesota."

"If, as you think, I'm intimate with Prisca, why would I want my wife back here? Wouldn't that crimp my style?"

"Not if Prisca was leaving in November after the election."

"You seem to have it all figured out. Why talk to me?"

"I'd like you to admit it. Save me time and money."

"Sorry, Miss Wright. You're going to have to earn this one." He stood, said, "Hope you have a good day", and walked out of the office. I followed to make sure the door closed behind him. With the castle secure, I returned to my desk.

Tina was back reading whatever it was she was reading on her iPad. I decided to build a fire in the fireplace and sit on the couch. There is something therapeutic in watching the flames and listening to the crackle of the burning wood. However, I'd no sooner gotten the fire going and was stretched out on the couch when the doorbell rang. In a moment, Bea announced Cal was on the doorstep. Tina stood, told me to see him, and vanished.

I got off the couch, told Bea to let him in, and went to my desk.

In a moment, Cal entered. "Hi, Harry." He cast a glance at Tina's desk and then returned his eyes to me. "I have the autopsy report I told Tina I'd give her."

"Hi, Cal, and thanks. She'll appreciate it, I'm sure."

He put the envelope on her desk. "I suppose it's over between Tina and me."

I motioned for him to take a seat and he did. "Don't give up hope. I think she still loves you. She's hurt and this is going to take awhile. Quite awhile."

He nodded. "I messed things up big time."

"Don't beat yourself up, Cal. Life happens. Tina's not the easiest person to be with."

He nodded again. There was a wistful look in his eyes.

"Have anything else for us?"

"We found a couple shell casings. Might identify who bought the gun. The ME confirmed it was a twenty-five caliber. Two bullets. Not hollow points. One smashed the window and grazed his forehead. The second entered near the corner of his left eye. The ME said it hit the back of his skull at an angle, followed the bone around, and made mincemeat of his brain."

"Probably didn't feel much, if anything."

"Yeah. The only saving grace. Any idea why he may have been shot?"

"My guess is he was a spy for Aagard's campaign."

"Tina share your opinion?"

"She hasn't said. She's focusing on two other people it looks for certain are leaking info to Aagard. That's what we're working on. Stopping the leak."

He nodded. "Well, I'd best be going. Thanks for sharing."

"No prob, Cal."

I walked him to the door and then went looking for Tina. She was in the library.

"Coast is clear," I said and returned to the office.

Tina was right behind me. She sat at her desk, opened the envelope, and looked at the ME report. After a minute she set it aside.

"Do you think Rossiter was the person on the phone?"

"Don't know, Tina. The voice was muffled."

She looked off into space. "If he was the one, do you think he had information to pass on to us about our moles?"

"Why would he? Why tell us?"

"To deflect suspicion from himself."

"I suppose that makes sense."

"We sink Horstman and Thoraldson and that takes eyes off him. However someone evidently did have eyes on him and killed him."

What she was saying made sense. I just wasn't sure that was what was going on. "I suppose it all hangs together. I wonder if Oberman is going to come through?"

"That's another possibility, Harry. Rossiter was just Oberman's errand boy."

"Possible. But then we'd know Rossiter was a spy. Why reveal him?"

"That is the question, isn't it?" She sat back in her chair, put her hands behind her head, and closed her eyes.

She stayed that way for some time. I heard no snoring and therefore assumed she was thinking. No sense for me to sit at my desk. Bea was watching the door and answering the phone. The fire was inviting. I moved to the couch in front of the fireplace and stretched out. The doorbell rang.

I got up and moved back to my desk. Bea poked her head in and said Prisca Thoraldson was in the waiting room. Tina sat up and told Bea to show her in.

When our guest was comfortably seated in the oversized oxblood wingback, she said, "I'm here. What do you want?"

"What's the nature of your relationship with Ted Horstman?" Tina asked.

"We're friends."

"How friendly are you?"

"What do you mean?"

"Are you engaging in sex with him?"

"God, you have a dirty mind. I said we're friends. I didn't say 'with benefits'."

"So nothing of benefit passes between you and Mr. Horstman?"

"Oh, I see. Now you're putting the finger on me, too."

"So tell me you're not passing information to Mr. Horstman."

"Okay. I'm not passing information to Mr. Horstman."

"Who is?"

"How the hell should I know? You're the expert. Expert at stealing people's money, if you ask me."

"What puzzles me, Ms. Thoraldson, is if everyone is so loyal to the Congresswoman, why would someone want to ruin her re-election bid? Alex Brewer should be the target, yet the Congresswoman is going to pay the price."

"I don't know."

"Don't know or won't tell?"

Prisca stood up and walked out of the office. I followed, but Bea had already beat me to closing the door behind our former guest. I returned to my desk.

"When are you bugging her office, Harry?"

"Tomorrow."

"Good. I'm tired of this case."

"Well, Sis, it's getting close to feeding time. I'll be in the kitchen."

"Tomorrow, after bugging Thoraldson's office, keep tailing Horstman."

"Will do. Right after my talk with Wikstrom."

"When is that?"

"Eight in the morning."

"God." There was a long pause. "I'll talk to Wikstrom. You get there early, plant that bug, and then tail Horstman."

"I'll be gone before you're even on the road."

I left, picked up my sous chef and headed for the kitchen. The time had come for me to interrogate a flounder.

16

BUGGED

Tuesday. September 30th

I was at Horstman's campaign headquarters very early. The sun wasn't even awake. However, at five-thirty in the morning no one else was either and the door was locked. I found a security person who at least looked awake and got him to let me into the office. He didn't want to, but when I took out my cell to call the Congresswoman, he capitulated. No sense in raising the ire of someone who might get you fired. At least I think that is what went through his mind.

Once inside, I went to Prisca's office and installed my little device on the side of her desk next to the wall. That way it had little to no chance of being detected. By quarter after six I was done, notified the guard I was finished so he could lock up, and was on my way to the Horstman residence to begin my day tailing Mr. Horstman around town.

Rush hour traffic is horrible. I hate it. The inevitable bumper-to-bumper. Thank goodness I'd hit the freeway at the very beginning of the impending traffic jam on my way to the campaign headquarters. From Eden Prairie to Minnetonka, where the

Horstman's lived, I took the city streets and was at Horstman's house by ten after seven.

The Focus does a pretty good job of blending in. There were a few cars parked on the street and that is always a plus, because you don't stick out that way. It looks very unusual when you're the only one. I parked a few doors down and waited for him to leave.

While waiting for Teddy to show, I listened to a podcast by M. Greenley Morton, the *Private Eye Extraordinaire*, on surveillance techniques. I wasn't learning anything new. His tips about the business of being a private eye are pretty routine and nothing special. The reason I listen is because he tells very interesting stories. Although the one he was telling on that particular podcast sounded an awful lot like the Flitcraft Parable from Hammett's *The Maltese Falcon*. Made me wonder if all his stories are made up or if he was just being lazy on that particular episode.

Along about eight-thirty, the BMW backed out of the drive and when he was a half-dozen car lengths ahead I pulled out and began following him. Nothing exciting, though, this morning. He drove straight to his office. I parked two rows behind and had a good view of both his car and the entrance to the office complex. And there I sat all morning.

At one, Ted got into his car and drove off. I followed. He went to the same restaurant we'd had lunch at and I'll give you three guesses whose car was in the lot and the first two won't count. If you guessed Prisca Thoraldson, you were right. I took photos of the cars, the cars with the restaurant in the background, and I even got a couple pictures of both cars in the same photo. Too bad I didn't have a couple bugs on me. I could have done David's job for him right then and there.

A little before three they left the restaurant. While following Horstman, I phoned in.

"Hey, Babe!"

"Harry! Is everything alright?"

"It is, Sweetums. Put me through to Tina."

"Okay. Love you! Bye!"

In a moment, I heard, "Yes, Harry?"

I gave her a synopsis of my morning and afternoon. "I'm following Horstman and one will get you ten he's driving to the hotel for dessert. You want me to keep shadowing him?"

"Is Thoraldson going back to campaign headquarters?"

"Don't know. I only have the for sure times she'll be out of her office."

"If they both show up at the hotel, wait, and then follow her when she leaves."

"Will do, Boss."

Tina disconnected and I followed Ted all the way to the Marriott. More pictures, an hour and a half wait, and then I followed Prisca to campaign headquarters. I called and activated the bug in her office. Maybe ten minutes passed before I heard a door close and then shortly after that Prisca's voice.

"Thanks again, Teddy, for lunch and the romp between the sheets. I'm really going to miss you when I move. You sure you won't change your mind?"

There was a bit of a pause and then, "I was just hoping, you know? I think we're good together and I'd love to have your babies and take care of you, like you should be taken care of. You're a wonderful man, Teddy."

More silence. Then, "That's too bad. Well, it's been fun. Yeah, sure, I'll keep getting you the information. I hate to hurt Mad—" A brief pause, followed by, "I know, I know. You get what you want and I get what I want." Another pause. "Okay, Baby, talk to you later."

There was the rustling of some papers and suddenly the sound stopped. "What the hell is this? Someone steal my mouse and leave me this clunky thing?"

The door opened and all was quiet.

I sat in my car thinking about what she said. I hadn't paid a lot of attention, but I seemed to recall she had a wireless keyboard and a wireless mouse. Did someone take her mouse and give her a cheaper one by means of replacement? Or did someone give her a bugged mouse to do the very thing I was doing?

———

I got home just as Bea and Tina were sitting down to eat supper and joined them.

Tina asked, "Anything?"

My reply was "office".

She nodded and launched into a discussion about places to retire. The reason being Bea wants to sell her house in Shoreview and buy a place where we'd like to live in retirement. Tina was arguing that very often the best place to retire is where you live. The point being she doesn't want us to move.

"But don't you want to live someplace warm and by the ocean?" Bea asked.

"This is home." Tina's tone of voice indicating her words were simply a different means of saying no.

Needless to say there was no consensus of opinion.

Supper finished and the cleanup done, we adjourned to the office with our tea and frozen custard. I think Tina's bowl had half a bottle of maraschino cherries on it.

"Well, Harry, what did you find out?"

I related what I'd heard Prisca say.

"That's it. Isn't it?" Bea said.

"Yes, it is, Bea," Tina answered. "However, I don't like her comment about the mouse. A bug can masquerade as a mouse. Maybe someone else decided to bug her."

"That's what I was thinking," I said.

"Do we know where Ms. Thoraldson is now?" Tina asked.

I checked my notes. "She's at a fundraiser."

"Where?"

"The Ambassador in Edina. The Congresswoman's to make a brief appearance. A couple of big shots are speaking. I think

Prisca's running the show. Don't really know when it ends. Started a half-hour ago."

Tina sat back in her chair, thought a moment, then leaned forward. "You've been out all day, Harry. I'm going to go over there. I don't like this. I don't like this at all."

"It's because of Rossiter, isn't it?" I said.

"Yes. Someone found out something, we're assuming it's that he was a spy, and killed him. Now it may be Prisca Thoraldson who's next."

"I can come along, Sis."

"No. I'll go. You've had a long day." She stood and walked out of the office.

Worry was all over Bea's face. "Harry, do you really think someone is going to kill Prisca Thoraldson?"

"Don't know. Tina's concerned enough to check the situation out herself. That in and of itself says something." And what it said was the Boss thought Prisca was in a lot of danger.

17

ONE LUCKY LADY

Wednesday. October 1st

WE GOT THE CALL AT TWENTY AFTER FOUR IN THE MORNING. WHEN I answered, the voice on the other end identified itself as belonging to Cal. That he identified himself was a good thing, because at that hour of the morning I'm generally good for nothing.

"Harry, you need to come down to HCMC as soon as possible."

"What happened?"

"Tina's been shot."

"Thanks. On my way."

Bea was looking at me. "What is it, Harry?"

"Come on, get dressed. We're going to Hennepin County Medical Center. Tina's been shot. That was Cal on the phone."

"Oh, my God! No!"

"Babe, get a grip. Come on."

She got out of bed and started pulling on a set of sweats. I was trying to button my shirt and tie my shoes all at the same time. Somehow I made it and when we were sufficiently presentable, we raced downstairs and out to the garage, got into Bea's Fiat, and she drove us downtown as if the Devil himself was in pursuit. She parked and we ran into the hospital.

The person at the Information Desk told us Tina was in surgery and we made a beeline to the waiting room. When we got there, Cal was sitting off by himself in a corner. He looked lost in thought. Bea ran to him and hugged him.

"What happened?" I asked.

"That's what I'm trying to figure out. I have Roberts interviewing anyone he can find. Seems there were a number of bystanders."

"Is he your new partner?" Bea asked.

"Yeah. Kevin Roberts. Been with me a couple months. Good guy."

"So what happened?"

"Looks like someone tried to take out..." He looked at his notebook. "A woman by the name of Prisca Thoraldson and a guy by the name of Theodore Horstman."

"Oh, my God!" Bea exclaimed.

"That guy is your client's husband. Right?"

I answered. "Yes. He's Congresswoman Madelyn Horstman's husband. Anyone killed?"

"Horstman is in bad shape. The shooter got him in the left eye at very close range. The woman took a round in her left shoulder and another in the left side of her neck. Again, at close range. Tina apparently tried to take down the attacker and got a bullet in her thigh. A second round was fired, which missed. Someone who apparently had a concealed carry permit was trying to get his forty-five out of the holster and the attacker put four bullets into him and ran off down the street. He died at the scene. A bullet must've severed an artery."

"Any description?" I asked.

"Tall. That's about it. Dark clothing. Waiting for forensics and the ME to get us their results. May I ask what Tina was doing there?"

"Where did the shooting take place?" I asked.

"At a bar called Jimmy's in Uptown."

I told Cal what we had uncovered concerning Ted and Prisca and Tina's concern someone might be after Prisca. He took the information and filed it away.

"Have you gotten any word on Tina?" Bea asked.

Cal shook his head. "Not since they took her into surgery. She was losing a fair amount of blood one of the beat cops said."

We sat and waited and, of course, waiting seems forever. Although I don't think we were sitting there for more than forty-five minutes. When Tina was wheeled out of surgery and put into recovery, the doctor came over to us.

Cal said, "This is Harry Wright. He's Justinia Wright's brother and this is his wife, Bea."

"Pleased to meet you," the doctor said. "I'm Doctor Abeler. Your sister was lucky, Mr. Wright. The bullet only nicked the femoral artery. If it had hit the artery full on, she wouldn't be with us. When she's stable, she'll be moved to her room and then you can see her. We'll keep her here for a few days to make sure everything is all right."

"Thanks, Doctor," I said.

He left and we waited some more, perhaps another half-hour before we were told the room she was going to be moved to.

"I think I'll be going," Cal said. "You'll keep me posted?"

We assured him we would and he left, looking for all the world like Atlas. The weight of the world on his shoulders.

"I feel sorry for Cal, Harry."

"Me, too, Babe."

Tina woke up a little past eight in the morning. She looked around, saw Bea and me, and said, "I guess I'm still alive. Unless you two died and went to hell with me."

"I'm not planning on going to hell, Sis. San Diego. The weather is better."

Tina smiled. "I'm not retiring there."

"Oh, shoot," Bea said and gave Tina a kiss on the cheek.

I held Tina's hand. "Glad you're with us, Sis."

"Thanks, you two. I'm glad I'm here. Wouldn't want to be anywhere else."

"Feel up to telling us what happened?" I asked.

"Not much to tell, actually. I went to Saint Louis Park and walked around the hotel where the fundraiser was being held. There was security there. Being part of the Congresswoman's team allowed me to get in. Nothing seemed out of place and when the formal part was over, I kept an eye on Thoraldson. I wanted to see what she'd do and to see if anyone else had his or her eye on her.

"When pretty much everyone had gone, she took off for downtown Minneapolis and I followed her all the way to Uptown. She parked and walked to Hennepin Avenue, where she met Horstman. I followed them to a bar, when out of nowhere someone shows up right behind them. Horstman and Thoraldson turned around and I heard gunfire. Horstman went down. Thoraldson tried to ward off the attack and the gun fired again and she went down.

"I was running to try and catch the assailant. The person must have heard me. He turned and I was close enough to try and deflect his arm. I did, but not enough. God, that bullet burned. I knew it wasn't good, because I was bleeding quite a bit. I tried putting pressure on the wound, when a woman came up and said she'd help. I lay down and she applied pressure until the paramedics arrived. Somewhere in there I heard more shots."

"Apparently someone tried to be a hero and died for it," I said.

"How did you find out?"

"Cal called us," Bea said.

I added, "He sat with us until the doctor said you were okay. He was very worried."

A cloud came over Tina's face.

"C'mon, Tina," I said, "the guy admitted he was a jerk. He cares about you."

She held up her hand. "Enough."

"You're beginning to sound like my ex."

"Harry. Don't cross the line."

I didn't say anything. Instead, I pushed a big, clunky chair into a corner of the room and sat in it. Bea sat on my lap. Tina sighed and rang for a nurse. After a moment, a woman appeared.

"What can I help you with?"

"My leg hurts."

"You're hooked up to a morphine drip. Just press this." The nurse showed her what button to press. "It will only dispense a couple drops. Doesn't matter how many times you push. Then you have to wait."

"What if it isn't enough?"

"Honey, you don't want too much of this. It'll constipate you right up."

"I don't give a shit."

"That so? Well, you take too much of that and I'll be giving you an enema so you can give a shit."

Tina glowered at the nurse.

"Anything else?"

Like a petulant child Tina said, no, and the nurse left. Then she looked at us.

"What are you two looking at?"

"You," I said.

"I'm tired." She closed her eyes and was soon asleep.

"She really has it in for Cal, doesn't she, Harry?"

"Tina can be unrelentingly unforgiving, Babe. His actions might have pushed her over the edge as far as he's concerned. And we can't forget what Cal did was rather cruel."

"It was, but he realizes he was wrong. It's just too bad. For both of them. They love each other."

"That it is, Babe. That it is."

There we sat and watched the Great Detective sleep. After a time, the doctor came in with a woman and one of the nurses, who woke Tina.

"You're a lucky lady, Ms. Wright. The bullet was small and just nicked the femoral artery. It missed bone and I don't think there was any major nerve damage. You should be up and walking with the help of a cane in no time at all. Any questions?"

Tina shook her head and the doctor, woman, and nurse left.

"Damn hospitals," Tina said. "Every time you go to sleep they wake you up." She closed her eyes and went back to sleep, only to have a nurse enter.

She looked at Tina, then shifted her gaze to us and asked, "Will she want lunch?"

"Probably," I said. "Leave me the menu and I'll call it in."

The nurse gave me the menu and left. I looked it over and ordered a meal for Tina. A little after noon the food arrived.

Once again she was woken and by the look on her face I knew she was going to be grumpy as hell. She looked at the tray, looked at me, and said, "You order this?"

"It was the best of the offerings."

A disgusted look crossed her face. "Cat food looks more appetizing." Nevertheless, she picked up the fork and began eating.

Bea went down to the cafeteria to get us something and came back with sandwiches. She handed me one and I unwrapped it. It looked a lot like colored styrofoam in between two pieces of white styrofoam. I took a bite. Yep, styrofoam masquerading as roast beef. I did swallow the stuff.

Before taking another bite, I asked, "Tina, do you think these shootings are all connected?"

She looked at the green stuff on her spoon. From where I was sitting, I think they were supposed to be green beans. She put the spoon down. "Yes. The question is what connects them. What connects Fishman, Rossiter, and now Horstman and Thoraldson?"

"The Congresswoman," I said.

"Exactly. Which means, at least I think it means, that the perpetrator is one of Horstman's campaign people. It's the only thing that makes sense."

There was a knock on the door and then a familiar face poked his head in.

"What the hell do you want, Swenson? Can't you leave me alone?"

"Look, Tina, uh, I mean Miss Wright, I have to ask you a few questions about what happened."

The look on her face would have turned the Medusa to stone. "Why you?"

"Because I'm the one handling this case."

"I don't want to talk to you."

Cal stood there. His face inscrutable.

I made a mental note to myself to never play poker with him.

What he said next was unexpected. "You don't want to forgive me, Wright? Fine. But you are going to answer my goddamn questions or I will throw the book at you for obstructing an investigation. I love you and treated you like shit. I'm sorry. It was the stupidest thing I've done. But right now I'm investigating a murder, two murders, and three attempted murders. And you are going to put your feelings about me aside and answer my questions."

Tina was mad. That much was obvious from looking at her. She stared at Cal and he at her. It was a marathon stare down. Three minutes and forty-seven seconds. This time Tina flinched.

"All right, Swenson, ask your questions."

"Thank you. Did you recognize the attacker?"

"No. I didn't get a good look at his face. He was wearing a hood."

"Can you describe the attacker?"

"Tall. Dressed in black. Even had black gloves. Face was hidden by the hood. Average frame, I think."

"Describe what happened."

Tina thought a moment before speaking. "I was following Thoraldson. Had tailed her from Saint Louis Park to downtown and then to Uptown, where she parked her car. I then followed her on foot to Hennepin. There she met up with Theodore Horstman. My guess was they had the meeting prearranged."

"What time was this?"

"Around one. The fundraiser was over at eleven, but there was a lot of lingering and Thoraldson was there. I suppose schmoozing the donors and potential donors. I stayed in the distance so as not to be seen."

"Did you see anyone else watching her?"

"No, I didn't. Apparently someone was."

"Where did they go when they met up on Hennepin?"

"They walked the several blocks to the bar."

"Jimmy's?"

"I believe that was the name. I think whoever's the shooter, must have known where Thoraldson was going because he was already in position. From out of nowhere he appeared right behind them. They turned around and then the shooting started."

"How far back were you?"

"Thirty, forty feet."

"What did you do when the shooting started?"

"I started running to catch the perp. Of course the sidewalk had people on it, so it wasn't a straight run. I was maybe five feet away when he turned around. I closed the gap enough and managed to hit his arm. The gun fired and I got hit. He fired again and missed. I was down and he took off. So I probably wasn't number one on his list."

Swenson nodded. "Anything else?"

"No."

"Any guesses as to who it might be?"

"You know I don't guess, Swenson. It's a fruitless endeavor."

A perturbed look flitted across his face. "Any suggestions on where to focus the search?"

"The campaign." She then gave him a summary of what the three of us had talked about before his arrival.

"Thanks, Wright. That's very helpful."

"You're welcome, Swenson."

"I might have to ask you more questions as new information comes to light."

There was a pause, long enough to be noticeable, before Tina spoke. "All right, Swenson. You know where to find me."

"I hope you're on your feet soon." He paused and then added, "I was worried sick about you. Just wanted you to know." He turned to us, said, "Harry, Bea," and left.

Tina pressed the morphine button. "I'd like to be alone, if you two don't mind."

"Sure, Sis. We'll be back in a little while."

Bea and I left. On the way to the car, Bea said, "They love each other. We just have to figure out how to get them together."

"Maybe we ought to let them figure it out."

"They won't. They need help and I'm going to help them."

18

JOB OFFER

Friday. October 3rd

We left the hospital with Tina shortly after noon. I drove the Flex so Tina would have room in the backseat. I'd made arrangements for a wheelchair rental and we had a couple canes. I also called to set up rehab appointments, but one will get you ten she won't go to more than one — if she goes at all.

Yesterday, Cal showed up just before lunch ostensibly to ask more questions. About five minutes into the questions, Tina interrupted.

"You're fishing, Swenson. You don't know your head from your ass and you want me to tell you which is which."

"Look, Wright, I'm just trying to get this mess straightened out. You have history with these jokers and I'm trying to figure out the truth from the bullshit and there's an awful lot of the latter flying around."

"You could talk to Harry."

Cal looked at me. "No offense, Harry." He turned his attention back to Tina. "He's the understudy and you're the prima donna."

Tina snorted her displeasure and finally agreed to hear him out. When he was done, she said, "You're making too many assumptions, Swenson. Gather the data, then analyze it. You know that. You getting pressure to solve this?"

"Yeah. The Congresswoman."

Tina nodded. "Self-righteous bitch."

"Right. Makes me want to change my party affiliation to 'None of the Above'."

A smile appeared on Tina's lips. "Now you know why I don't vote." Then she suddenly remembered Cal was her worst enemy. "You done? I'm tired."

"Yeah, sure. Thanks, Wright."

When Cal had gone, Tina blurted out, "That man. What part of *no* does he not understand?"

Bea said, "He loves you and you love him."

"That's enough out of you, Mrs. Wright. You marry the son of a bitch."

Yep. Still just a wee bit unforgiving is our Great Detective.

Today, however, was quieter. No Cal and Tina was discharged. She was actually upbeat and talked all the way home about writing her own piano transcription of Beethoven's Fifth Symphony. I swung by Jakeeno's and picked up lunch: a sausage, garlic, onion, and sauerkraut pizza for Tina, the House Special for Bea, and the Vegetarian Special for moi.

When we reached the pile we call home, I dropped Tina off at the door and she hobbled into the house using the canes, the "goddamn wheelchair" being for cripples. She got settled on the couch in the living room and we ate our pizza there. Tina and I had Seyval Blanc to drink and Bea had water. Lunchtime conversation bounced from healthcare to education to our foreign military adventures. I won't bore you with the details. I'm sure you have your own opinions.

We were in a pizza-induced euphoria when the doorbell rang.

"I'll get it," Bea said.

In a moment, she came back. "Chelsea Lindstrom is in the waiting room. She's Alex Brewer's assistant, right?"

I confirmed that was true.

"She's here on behalf of the campaign."

A frown clouded Tina's face. She was facing a dilemma. With restricted mobility, she didn't want to make the little trip to the office. Her policy, however, was no business discussed outside the office. I felt a bit sorry for her. She's a big one for routine and now it was obvious her routine was going to go through a major shakeup. And by the look on her face it was equally obvious she didn't like it one bit. When she finally spoke, the words confirmed my hypothesis. "If I catch the bastard who shot me, I'll kill him. With my bare hands. Bring her here."

Bea retrieved Chelsea Lindstrom and brought her to the living room, where I introduced her to Miss Justinia Wright.

"Miss Wright and I have already met."

I brought up a chair for her to sit in, making sure it was positioned so Tina didn't have to turn her head.

"I'm sorry about your injury," Chelsea said. "Hopefully you'll heal soon."

"Thank you," Tina murmured.

"Miss Wright, I'm here to ask you to become an official part of Congresswoman Horstman's campaign. We'd like you to be the Security Director."

"Not interested."

"But the campaign needs you. It's in complete disarray and your work as the special consultant gives you an advantage. Mad's spending all of her time sitting by her husband and Alex is making *all* of the decisions on her own. I'm going out on a limb here and I hope you don't say anything, but, well, pardon my saying so, but she pisses off a lot of people."

"That's the Congresswoman's problem. Not mine. When you think people can walk on water, you have to put up with the waves when they don't."

"Mad could lose. Don't you care?"

"No, I don't. I'm apolitical."

"Oh. I thought... Well, I guess it doesn't matter what I thought. Okay, well, uh, thank you for your time."

"Who asked you to offer me this job?"

"Alex, herself."

Tina said nothing. Just stared off into space.

Chelsea stood.

"Before you go." Tina shifted slightly and winced. "Where was Alex Brewer yesterday during the fundraiser?"

"She was there."

"I didn't see her."

"She was there early, before everything started. She was there when Mad spoke." Chelsea paused. "Hm. Now that you mention it, I don't recall seeing her after Mad spoke. But I was busy helping out and wasn't paying a lot of attention to who was where."

"Thank you, Ms. Lindstrom. None of you pressured Ms. Brewer to offer me the position?"

"It was mentioned in one of our meetings and everyone thought it a good idea."

"I see."

"Again, sorry about the injury."

"Thank you."

Bea escorted the assistant campaign manager to the door and returned to the dining room. Tina lay back on the couch.

"We'll let you sleep, Sis."

"Thanks, Harry." She sat up. "Oh, while I'm thinking of it. I did talk to Wikstrom on Tuesday. With the deaths, she's coming around to believing there is indeed a spy. As to who it is, she had no idea. But thought the new people, the ones who hadn't been with the Congresswoman that long were the most likely."

"Why's that," I asked.

"They haven't had the time to gain loyalty."

"If that's the case, then Rossiter, Littlewood, Vi Nguyen, Lindstrom, and Felder would be the likely candidates according to her."

"True. We suspect Rossiter out of that bunch. I think the others are in the clear after Tuesday night's shooting."

"Did you ask about who might want Rossiter dead?"

"I did. She had no idea." Tina lay back down.

"You get some sleep, Sis."

"Thanks."

Bea and I went to the game room and racked up the balls on the pool table.

"Harry, why did Tina ask about Alex?"

"I don't know. That she did, I would say doesn't bode well for Alex. Then again, maybe Tina just wanted to know."

Bea was well on her way to skunking me in our pool game when I was saved by the doorbell. I went to see who it was and saw David Nagasawa on our porch with a bouquet of flowers in his hand. I threw open the door and invited him in. Bea arrived and all three of us went to the Inner Sanctum.

"How's Miss Wright doing? These are for her, by the way."

"That was very thoughtful of you, David," Bea said, while taking the bouquet from him. She left, saying she was going to put the flowers in a vase.

"She's doing well, David, thanks. She's resting now."

"I heard on the police scanner about the shooting. I thought I'd wait till she got home to stop by."

Bea returned with the flowers and put the vase on Tina's desk.

"Unfortunately, I wasn't able to do much to accomplish the job she wanted me to do. Security is too tight on both Horstman's and Thoraldson's residences. I was able to bug their cars. I didn't try Theodore Horstman's office once I heard about the shooting."

"That's okay, David," I said, "I don't think the poor devil is going to make it."

David nodded his head in agreement. "I heard through the grapevine he's brain dead."

"Oh, dear," Bea said.

David added, "I guess they're waiting on the Congresswoman to give the okay to pull the plug."

Bea wiped her eyes. "That's so sad."

"It is. Well, Harry, let Miss Wright know what I told you. I don't see any reason to pursue it, but she's the boss."

"Will do, David. She's sleeping, otherwise I'd have taken you to her, so you could tell her in person."

"Understand."

"Send me your time."

"I will."

The three of us walked to the front door and said our good-byes. David left and Bea and I returned to the game room. In the back of my mind, I was wondering if Brewer was next on the list to receive a bug.

19

IT MAKES NO SENSE

Saturday Morning into Afternoon. October 4th

TINA DOESN'T LIKE HER ROUTINE MESSED WITH. THE SITUATION WAS bad enough she had to eat in the living room yesterday, the doctor advising against a lot of walking, but to sleep there as well must've been the proverbial straw breaking the camel's back. Because when breakfast was ready, into the dining room she hobbled. She'd probably told herself, damn the bullet wound, the routine must be saved.

I told her I'd have been more than happy to serve her in the living room. Her reply confirmed my guess: "No. We eat in the dining room."

Bea entered and the seven of us, humans, dog, and cats, settled into our usual routine. Although I doubt the four-legged people ever varied from it. Things were so much back to normal, Tina even harangued Bea and I to wash our hands after reading the paper. I guess there is a lot to be said in favor of routine after all. It's comforting.

When we were finished eating, Tina hobbled her way to the office. Yes sirree Bob, back to normal. Bea and I cleaned up the dishes and then she got ready to go grocery shopping, while I made my way to the office. When I got there, Tina had a cigar going and a glass of madeira poured.

She sent a cloud of smoke to the ceiling. "God, it's good to be home. Pretty flowers. She looked at the card and smiled."

I reported what David had told me. She simply nodded and took a sip of madeira.

"So now what?" I prodded.

"For crying out loud, Harry. I'm wounded."

All I could do was roll my eyes. "So does that mean I get paid for doing nothing?"

She puffed on her cigar and followed up with a sip of madeira. "No. Go down to the campaign headquarters and find out whatever you can."

"Such as?"

"Whatever. I won't know if it's useful until you tell me what you find."

"I see. You just don't want me bugging you."

"You said it. I didn't."

"Okay. Fine."

"And I want you to find out if Swenson knows anything about what was in Fishman's safes."

I grabbed my hat and jacket, left a note for Bea, and decided to take the Maserati for a spin. Traffic wasn't too bad for a Saturday morning, which enabled me to make good time. I parked and took the elevator to the headquarters on the fifth floor.

When I entered, Opal, the receptionist, was at her desk. She put on a brave face, but clearly it was a mask.

"Good morning, Mr. Wright."

"Good morning, Opal. I'm here to look around."

"Not many people are here."

"Any word on Mr. Horstman?"

She nodded and tears started to fall. "Mad let them pull the plug. He died early this morning."

"Sorry to hear that. Is Alex around?"

"She's with Mad."

"Makes sense. Alex must be a great comfort to the Congresswoman."

"Oh, she is. Mad would be lost without her."

"See you later, Opal."

"Bye, Mr. Wright."

My first stop was Prisca's office to remove the bug I'd placed and take a look at her mouse.

Opal was right. Not many people were around. All of the offices except for Vi's and Darius's were dark. Eight people were on the phones. The time seemed a bit early to be running a phone bank, although with everything going on of late maybe they needed to assure potential voters the Congresswoman was still in the race.

I removed the bug and looked at the mouse. Wireless. Either Prisca had gotten her mouse back or someone had made the switch back to the original. In either case, I wasn't able to verify if the "clunky" mouse was a bug or not.

Finished with Prisca, I stepped outside her office and looked over the floor. My eye caught Jawanda Clark's nameplate. I didn't envy her her job as Communications Director one bit. Damage control must be sucking up thirty hours a day. Susan Wikstrom's door was closed. I didn't envy her her job either. Trying to hold the precincts together with all the bad press was a labor of Hercules.

Darius Littlewood, the IT man, was in his office playing his keyboard like a jazz musician playing a solo. Vi Nguyen, however, didn't look busy at all. Her door was open and I took the liberty of poking my head in.

"Hi, Harry. Come on in."

I entered and took a seat. "I certainly don't envy any of the campaign directors. It must be a nightmare."

"It is. Although Jawanda thinks we might be able to get a sizable sympathy vote. Susan, though, isn't so sure. The murders are scaring off the grassroots support."

"What about donations?"

"Chelsea's taken over that job. Some of the donors have the jitters. She's trying her best to make sure they don't leave us."

"Who's taken over Rossiter's job?"

"I'm doing what I can on that one. Don't really have a clue what to do. Chelsea helps when she can. Although Mad hasn't been doing any speaking, so things have been quiet. I suppose that will change now after the funeral. Any closer to finding out who's leaking the information?"

"Still working on it."

"Does that mean you don't know or aren't telling?"

"It means I'm not admitting to either one."

She laughed. "Were you a lawyer?"

"No. College professor."

"Really?"

"Yep."

"What subject?"

"Philosophy and history."

"Mind if I ask how you came to be a private detective?"

"Budget cuts sacked my position and my sister offered me a job."

"You married?"

"Yes. Just recently."

"Congratulations."

"Thanks."

"Do you like being a detective better than being a teacher?"

"In a perfect world, I'd rather be teaching. But being a detective with my sister has its perks. What happens to you when the campaign is over?"

"If Mad wins, I go to Washington. If she loses, I go back to private practice."

"Is Alex going to be back today?"

"Don't know. She's with Mad. Supporting her. God knows the poor woman needs it."

"Any word on Prisca?"

"The first bullet hit bone in her shoulder, we were told. Apparently there was a lot of damage caused by bone fragments. The second bullet in her neck caused nerve damage. The doctors don't know the full extent or how permanent it will be."

"Major bummer, that."

"Yeah. Guess she's lucky to be alive, although maybe it would have been better had she died."

"Why do you say that?"

"She might have permanent paralysis. And that has to suck."

"S'pose so. No idea if she'll be coming back to the campaign then?"

"I'd guess no."

I nodded. In my mind I couldn't help but think whoever'd shot Horstman and Prisca had beaten us in the detection game and stopped the leak in a very effective manner. It also meant we hadn't earned the money we'd gotten. Although, I doubted Tina would willingly return any of it.

"I'll be shoving off, Vi. Thanks."

"Bye, Harry."

I left Vi's office and on the way out confirmed with Opal the phone number for Alex and asked if she had any idea when the campaign manager would be in. She didn't know. I thanked her and left.

On my way to my car, I ran over the list of campaign staff. None of them liked Brewer.

They'd fingered Prisca as the mole and would have fired her except they were scared they'd lose donors. Did Prisca actually have that much influence over the donors? Apparently the others thought so.

By shooting her, she was no longer a problem. But why shoot Ted Horstman? Who stood to gain from his death? That made no sense to me. Shooting him could potentially drive the Congresswoman to give up the campaign. And no one wanted that.

None of it made sense. At least to me.

Although, it obviously made sense to the shooter.

Tina always harps on motive. So what was the motive in this

case? The simple answer would've been to fire Prisca. But they didn't.

Someone, though, bugged the offices. At least Prisca's and presumably Rossiter's. So why the murder and attempted murder? Why not just fire them? Which means I also didn't understand hiring us.

Why spend two hundred K when they could just as well have fired the suspects? The whole thing made no sense whatsoever.

I got in my car and called Cal, asking him, when he answered, if he had anything on the contents of Fishman's safes. He said he'd check and get back to me. I started the Maserati, listened to the engine purr for a minute, put it in gear, and drove home.

Along about now what seemed to make the most sense to me was a martini. In fact, that made an awful lot of sense.

20

A CHANGE OF SCENERY

Saturday Evening. October 4th

WHEN I GOT HOME, BEA WAS MAKING SUPPER. I GAVE HER A KISS AND made myself a martini.

"Rough day, Harry?"

"This case is enough to induce a coma. My brain hurts."

"That ought to take the edge off."

I held up the glass. "It will indeed. Might even need two."

"I'd be under the table just smelling it."

I laughed. "That you would, Babe." Bea has a low tolerance to alcohol. Tina says it's because she's too skinny.

"Tina's in the office."

"Thanks, Babe." I took myself and the martini to the Inner Sanctum.

Tina looked up from her book when I entered. "A martini? You don't drink martinis. Is this a new routine?"

"Nope. Just need to numb the brain before it fries out asking 'why?'."

"Talk to me."

I told her about my day at the campaign headquarters and my

ruminations. She nodded her head along the way to show she was listening and smiled a couple times when I told her what was puzzling me about the case.

Tina put a bookmark in the book and leaned back in her chair. "Once, when I was in Vitebsk, I had an interesting encounter. I was posing as an artist painting a series of eastern European landscapes. In reality, I was a handler for a Byelorussian who was working for us.

"One day the agent comes to me and gives me the code phrase indicating he had a delivery for me. That night I went to one of the local nightclubs where I was to pick up the package. I sat in a booth, positioning my wine glass so it could easily be seen by someone entering the club. After awhile, a man comes up to me and gives me the password. He's the package. I invite him to sit, we make small talk for awhile, and then leave the nightclub. We walk for a little bit and then I ask him what he wants.

"He tells me he wants asylum in the West. I ask why and he says, 'I want a change of scenery.' I ask more questions. The man, I'll call him Ivan, is the chief engineer on a top secret Russian robotics program. He's married and has two children. I tell him we probably won't be able to get his family out. He says he understands and he's looking for a change of scenery anyway.

"That bothers me. I invite Ivan to stay with me, in case the Russians were after him. He assured me they weren't, he was on holiday. I contacted my superior in Minsk. Come to find out Ivan was in fact who he said he was and my boss was very excited at 'our little coup'. How the 'our' crept in there puzzled me. *He* had nothing to do with finding him.

"Anyway, in the time Ivan was with me I was unable to ferret out a reason for his defection. He was happily married, loved his kids, was well paid, and highly valued. He had everything anyone could want. There was no motive other than the mysterious desire for a change of scenery."

"Did you ever find out his reason?"

"No. Arrangements were made for his move to the States and he was out of my life."

"So what does this have to do with our case?"

"Think about it. I'm sure the philosophy professor will figure it out." And she went back to her book.

As for me, I had a second martini.

21

BREWER

Sunday Morning. October 5th

I WAS LISTENING TO VAUGHAN WILLIAMS'S *MASS IN G MINOR* WHILE making breakfast. The cats and dog got first dibs on my time, the bipedal critters taking second fiddle. However I was the only biped up, so I guess in the end it didn't matter.

Religion isn't my thing. However, sacred music has a very strong effect on me. I think it's the hope and comfort so often expressed. Mythology aside, there is something to be said for maintaining hope in something better and taking comfort in what we can.

You might be wondering what I could possibly take hope and comfort in if I don't buy into religion. It's quite simple. I take hope and comfort in the fact that life is what I make it. Therefore, I hope for the best, prepare for the worst, and take comfort in the fact that I am free as long as no one controls my mind.

Seneca once wrote, Life, like a story, isn't dependent on length to be good, but on quality. I have no regrets. I live a good life. I take comfort in that and all of the things and people I've been blessed with. And every act of good I see and do gives me hope there are a lot of people like myself who try to make this a better place.

Now you might also be wondering about this philosophical discursion. To be honest, I made that little detour because I didn't want to talk about the case.

You all probably have figured out who the perp is. I, however, was totally at sea and Tina was milking being shot for all she could in order to get out of work. My job is mainly getting Tina to work and thereby making sure the client gets what he or she paid for. Thus far, the murderer was doing our job for us. Very frustrating that.

In the middle of my musing and breakfast prep, the doorbell rang. I wiped my hands and went to the door. On the porch, was Lieutenant Cal Swenson. I threw the door open.

"Greetings, Cal. Come in."

"Hi, Harry. Got some news for you from the ME."

I guided him to the outer office, our waiting area, and where Bea's desk is.

"Making any progress, Cal?"

"Not much. They're a tough bunch."

"Horstman's campaign staff?"

"Yes. The ME confirmed all were shot with a .25 ACP pistol. Forensics confirmed the same pistol used against Rossiter was used in the attack outside the bar. And was also used on Simon Fishman. It's now a quadruple homicide as Theodore Horstman died."

"I heard."

"Oh, I checked on Fishman. The safes were clean. Nothing in them."

"Which means whoever killed him must've gotten the combinations and taken whatever was in there."

"That is what we're assuming. Although it is possible there was nothing in them to begin with. No prints other than Fishman's. Has Tina gotten anywhere?"

"If she has, she hasn't told me. And I'm completely at sea."

"Makes for two of us. Reason dictates the perp is someone working for the campaign. Can't find a motive or anyone with opportunity."

"What about Brewer?"

"Can't put her at the scene and her significant other alibis her."

I thought about that and also thought about the comment Vi Nguyen had made concerning Abba. "And I suppose you can't find a hole in the wife's alibi."

"Nope. Brewer alibis her."

"They're a tough bunch of nuts."

"That they are. Well, I'll be going. I suppose you're making breakfast."

"I am."

A wistful look appeared in his eyes and then it passed. I walked him to the door and then returned to the kitchen. Bea was up.

"You just missed Cal. Had some info for us."

"Wish he could've stayed."

"I think he was thinking the same thing. Not today, though."

My sweetie and I finished preparing breakfast together and moved it to the dining room table. Tina joined us as we sat down.

"Who rang the doorbell?" she asked.

"Cal. Gave us some info."

She nodded and buried her nose in her iPad.

After breakfast, Bea went to retrieve the vacuum sweeper and Tina and I moved to the office, where I reported what Cal had told me. She merely nodded and picked up her book.

"Are we done with this case?" I asked.

"No."

"So what's next? We have those volunteers Brewer doesn't like."

She closed the book on a finger. "Forget them for now. Bug Brewer's office."

The clock on my desk told me the time was nine-thirty. I

thought about how to proceed and decided the best way would be to just bulldog ahead.

"I'll be back later." If Tina was listening, she didn't acknowledge. I took off, assuming she had heard what I said, found Bea and kissed her goodbye, got into the Maserati and drove out to the campaign headquarters.

I hadn't driven the car that much in the entire time I'd owned it. Nice car. I'm going to have to put it in the regular rotation.

When I arrived at the campaign headquarters, I was in luck. Only Opal was holding down the fort. Everyone else was at the memorial service for Ted Horstman. I told her there were some things I needed to check out and in I went.

Brewer's office was spare. Desk, phone, computer, filing cabinets, two extra chairs, and a map of the district on the wall. Her desk was in the center of the room and was more like a table than a traditional desk. I placed the bug underneath and out of the way of her legs. I walked around the front and stooped down so I was about the same height as most of the women. Couldn't see it. Sat in one of the chairs. Couldn't see it. We were good. I noted the number on Brewer's desk phone.

Out to the parking lot, where I activated the bug and called Brewer's number. The ringing came through loud and clear. We had reception. I drove back home and reported to Tina.

"Good. Call Ed, Gwen, and David. Have them tail Brewer."

"Okay, consider it done. What should I do?"

"Monitor the bug."

"What are you going to do?"

"Dock your pay if you don't quit asking me questions."

Needless to say, I shut up. After all, she's the genius. I'm just the flunky. Brewer was in Tina's sights. My guess was Tina was confident she was going to find something the police couldn't. But what, I still didn't know.

22

MRS F. TENNYSON JESSE

Sunday Night. October 5th

ALL WAS QUIET IN BREWER'S OFFICE AT THE CAMPAIGN headquarters. Gwen had called in to report Alex was at the Horstman residence and had been there ever since the memorial service. Gwen was relieved by Ed and he too reported no change. Along about eight, Tina looked up from her book.

"Call Jim Oberman. I'd like him to stop by tomorrow."

"Isn't he a bit old hat now?"

"Maybe. I'd like to see him anyway."

"Okay." I picked up my desk phone and dialed the Aagard campaign's number and when the phone was answered, asked to speak to Jim Oberman. There was some hesitation. I gave the person my name and told him to quit dawdling. A lot of money was at stake. I figured if I mentioned money that ought to get results and it did. Within a minute or two Oberman was on the phone.

"Mr. Wright, what can I do for you?"

"Justinia Wright misses you and would like to see you tomorrow."

"Well, uh, I'm not sure—"

"Of course you're sure. Scandal isn't something you want plaguing *your* campaign right now is it?"

"No, it isn't. Any particular time?"

"When's most convenient for you?"

"Ten o'clock tomorrow morning would work."

"See you then, Mr. Oberman. Don't be late."

I hung up the phone. "Mission accomplished, Sis."

"Good."

"What does Oberman have to do with anything? If he'd wanted to play ball, he would have done so by now."

"I'm not interested in that. I want confirmation on a few points. Nice maneuver to get to talk to him and nice play to get him to come here. You're learning quite nicely, Harry."

"Gee, thanks. Never mind that I just lied my way through the whole thing."

"Not so. A lot of money *was* at stake. No lie there. And we have dirt Horstman could use. No lie there either. Both statements were true. One was simply out of context and the other involved an implied potential course of action. He *assumed* we'd follow through. But you know I'm apolitical and don't give a rat's ass about either campaign."

"I feel much better. Thanks, Sis." Too bad there's not an emoticon for sarcasm. Then, again, maybe there is. I should look it up. Tina, however, ignored me and went back to her book.

Bea was sitting on the loveseat in front of the fireplace and laughing at Tina and me. At least that is what I assumed. I got up from my desk and sat next to her. She returned to her tatting and I just stared at the flames, letting my mind chew through the data. My thoughts drifted back to Tina's favorite criminologist: Mrs F. Tennyson Jesse. The six motives for murder: gain, revenge, elimination, jealousy, lust of killing, and conviction. I also thought of Mrs. Jesse's statement, "Most criminals are great egoists and inordinately vain, but these two qualities are found to excess in murderers."

I turned to Tina. "Was the Congresswoman inordinately vain and a great egoist?"

She looked up from her book, a smile on her lips. "Yes. She's a politician."

I paused a moment. What would Mad's motive be? Elimination? Getting rid of the people compromising her campaign? Could she have killed her own husband? I asked Tina.

"Anybody can kill anybody under the right circumstances."

"That doesn't answer my question."

"Ask her yourself. I've been shot."

"Oh, for crying out loud. Give it a rest already."

"Maybe I should shoot you. Then I'd get some sympathy."

"You don't have a twenty-five."

"You don't know what I have."

That one stopped me. The storage garage. She's right. I didn't know what was out there other than a vintage Alfa Romeo and now the Lamborghini. Then, again, that might be all that's out there.

"Fine, Tina. I'll ask her myself."

"You're busy monitoring the bug."

"Okay, I won't ask her."

"Now can I get back to my book?"

"Sure. Sorry for disturbing you. Thank God they didn't have to amputate."

Bea started laughing again and Tina's smirk was turned towards her book.

23

SALAMI TACTICS

Monday. October 6th

TINA WAS HER USUAL GRUMPY SELF THIS MORNING AT BREAKFAST. Getting shot hadn't changed that one bit. She drank her cup of tea, ate a slice of toast with butter, drank a second cup, ate another slice of toast with orange marmalade, and then hobbled off to the office. Bea and I also had tea and toast. However, we added soft-boiled eggs to ours.

After we cleaned up the dishes, we went to the office. Bea took up her post as receptionist and I went on into the Inner Sanctum where I waited upon the high priestess and did her bidding, which today was quite simple. I monitored the bug. And it was mostly quiet. I picked up some faint sounds early, which I figured were voices from their morning meeting. Unfortunately, I couldn't make out any of the words.

At quarter to ten, I heard noise. Paper rustling, file cabinet drawer opening and closing. Then I heard a voice. Sounded like Jawanda's.

"Are we good on the press release? I sent it to you yesterday."

"Yes, it's fine." That was Brewer's voice.

There was the rustling of paper, typing on the keyboard, and then silence.

The doorbell rang and in a moment Bea was ushering in Jim Oberman. I set the headphones aside. He sat in the oversized oxblood wingback and said, "I'm here. What do you want?"

Tina observed him for a few seconds before speaking. "Why didn't you get back to me?"

"Lost interest in your offer."

"Why?"

"I don't see where that is your business."

"I can find out."

"I doubt it."

"There's nothing more uncertain than a dead sure thing."

He shrugged. "If it's so important to you, then find out."

"I'm sorry about Rossiter."

His eyes narrowed, he tensed up, and suddenly relaxed. "Yes. Very sad. A tragedy. He was young and had promise."

"Did you plant him before or after contact with Horstman? Ted Horstman."

"Don't know what you're talking about."

"Of course you do, Mr. Oberman. I know Horstman was passing his wife's campaign information to you."

"If you say so."

"I do. I'd like to know if he was the chicken or the egg."

"You sure want an awful lot of stuff for free. Remember, you get what you pay for."

"You ever hear of Mátyás Rákasi?"

"No."

"He was head of the Hungarian Communist Party and was the one who coined the term *salami tactics*. He said he cut off the opposition like slices off of a salami."

"And this is important why?"

"I'd hate to think what Mr. Aagard would say when it becomes public knowledge his Communications Director was engaging in a political strategy practiced by Communists."

"You are trying to blackmail me."

"Blackmail only occurs when I have something of yours you don't want others to know about. It's obvious to me you are an upstanding member of the Republican Party and therefore have nothing to hide."

"God, you fight dirty."

"How can I 'fight dirty', as you say, if you've nothing to hide? I can only 'fight dirty' if you have something you need to hide. Do you have something you need to hide, Mr. Oberman?"

"What is it you want?"

"An answer to my question concerning Ted Horstman."

He took a deep breath and exhaled. "We had Rossiter in place when Ted Horstman came to us after the primary campaign. He'd passed information to Fishman and, since Fishman had lost, he now wanted to pass information to us. He wanted his wife out of Washington and, since he couldn't persuade her, he wanted her to lose."

"Let me guess. Horstman gave you information and you, in turn, had Rossiter pass on false information."

"Yes. Rossiter's job was to get allies against Brewer, who is, by the way, a pretty shrewd manager, to destroy the campaign through infighting. He didn't have to work too hard at it, though. Brewer's doing a fine job on her own."

Tina steepled her fingers. "I would guess he passed on a lot of information to Jawanda Clark, Horstman's Communications Director."

"He did. She's not bad at the communications piece. Not so good on the research. Damon provided her with information, let her take credit for finding it, and she was thankful."

"Thank you, Mr. Oberman."

"This stays with you?"

"I don't see why not."

"Good. Goodbye, Miss Wright."

He got up and left.

"Salami tactics?" I said.

"Yes. That's what Rákasi called it."

"Huh. That piece of history I didn't know. Someone should make a political video game. They could call it *The Salami Game*."

"It already exists in reality. It's called the political process."

24

TERMINATED

Monday Night. October 6th

For supper, I made a beef roast with Yorkshire Pudding, oven roasted potatoes with rosemary, sherried puree of peas, a lettuce salad, and mince pie for dessert. Hopefully the roast beef would make Tina's little meat-loving heart jump for joy.

Our supper conversation went from the typhoon that hit Tokyo to the Hong Kong pro-democracy demonstrations to the Ebola epidemic. Lots of problems in the world, yet we were eating roast beef and had mince pie for dessert. Of course, we ignored the Horstman campaign murders because they were business and business wasn't discussed in the dining room.

With supper safely stowed away, and dishes cleaned up, we adjourned to the office. Tina and I settled in at our desks and Bea did the same on the chesterfield.

All day long it was nothing out of the ordinary. Only routine chatter came across the bug. In succession, David, Gwen, and Ed had reported nothing more than routine movements on the part of Alex Brewer. I was just about to ask a question, when the phone rang. I answered.

"Wright Investigations."

"Is this Harry Wright?"

"It is."

"Hi, Harry. This is Vi Nguyen from Congresswoman Horstman's campaign."

"Hi, Vi. How are you?"

"I'm fine, Harry. And you?"

"Likewise."

"That's good. Say, Alex Brewer asked me to call. She's terminating our contract with you."

"Just a minute, Vi. I'm putting you on speaker so Miss Wright can hear." I flipped a switch. "Okay, as you were saying."

"Hi, Miss Wright. This is Vi Nguyen. Alex Brewer, on behalf of the campaign, is terminating the contract between you and the campaign."

Tina leaned back in her chair. "Why?"

"Because we've determined there's no longer a leak and therefore no longer a need for your services."

"I see. And how has she determined this?"

"I don't know. I'm assuming it's based on information Alex has. Anyway, she told me to call and I'm calling."

"Very well." The look on Tina's face wasn't pleasant.

"There's one other thing. She's asking you to return all of the money except for your time and expenses."

Tina knit her eyebrows. "That wasn't the agreement. The agreement was a flat fee of two hundred thousand in cash."

"Yes, for you to get information from the late Simon Fishman and to find who was leaking information to Aagard's camp. You've done neither. Therefore, you've not fulfilled the terms of the contract and since the campaign has determined there's no longer a leak, you aren't entitled to the money. Alex is allowing you reasonable compensation."

Tina sat back in her chair. Her face showed she was suffering from an acute case of exasperation. "Ms. Nguyen, the contract clearly stipulates the fee is for my time and expenses and results are not guaranteed. However, as I noted to Ms. Brewer, I do get results. I also noted the results may not be to her or anyone on the campaign's liking. I can produce evidence Simon Fishman was no longer in possession of the information Alex Brewer and Congresswoman Horstman believed he had and that this was the situation within just a few hours of his death. I am also in possession of evidence identifying who the moles were and when I discovered them. And since both results were prior to my termination, if the campaign has determined there is no longer a leak, I can only assume my actions are in part responsible. Therefore, I am entitled to the money and intend to keep it."

"I see. Why didn't you say something?"

"That, Ms. Nguyen, was my prerogative. I had not finished investigating. However, now that my services have been terminated, I will write up my report and send it to Alex Brewer. If she still insists on the money being returned, then the campaign will have to sue me."

There was silence. After a moment, Vi spoke. "It would have been helpful to have had a progress report."

It seemed to me, Vi was grasping at non-existent straws. Tina plowed on. "The contract did not include a specific report schedule. I said nothing because I was not sure I'd found all of the moles. Apparently I have. I'm entitled to the money and will not be returning it."

"Okay. We'll wait for your report. Bye Miss Wright, Harry." And a dial tone sounded.

I hung up the phone.

"Call off David, Gwen, and Ed. I want their reports pronto. See if you can retrieve the bug tomorrow. If not, we'll have to leave it. She didn't say to turn the badges in. Do so tomorrow. That will give you an excuse to visit the headquarters. As for now, shut the bug off."

There was a frown on my face. "Rather odd, don't you think, Tina? Alex was just asking you to join the campaign."

"Yes. Then again, if she couldn't have me working for her it is most likely in her best interests to distance me as much as possible. Anyway, thank God we're done with this case. It's been nothing but one big conspiracy game. Although I'm peeved I won't be able to track down who shot me."

I liked that. The Conspiracy Game. Come tomorrow, I was going to have to conspire on the best way to retrieve that bug.

25

THE ENEMY OF MY ENEMY

Tuesday. October 7th

In the morning, I was at Horstman campaign headquarters just before nine.

"Hi Opal. I want to turn in my and Miss Wright's badges. Who should I see about that?"

"You can leave them with me."

"Might I say goodbye to a few people?"

"I'm sorry, Mr. Wright. Alex Brewer said you and Miss Wright were not allowed in unless accompanied by a staffer."

"I see. Well, then, here you go." I gave her the badges and bid her a good day.

Outside the headquarters, facing the elevator, I turned to my right to check out the other suites.

There was a corridor running the length of the building. There were several doors visible and one I was specifically looking for. The restroom.

I also spotted the other thing I was looking for. The fire alarm.

The restroom had one person in it. I waited until he left, then using a paper tissue so no fingerprints would show, pulled the fire alarm and ran into the bathroom.

I crouched on top of a toilet and bolted the door to the stall. That way, should anyone check the restroom, they wouldn't see my feet and assume no one was there.

The alarm siren was screaming and I heard the rush of people trying to get out of the building.

When the noise died down, I left the stall and listened at the door. When I heard nothing, I entered the empty corridor and made a beeline to the campaign headquarters.

The door was not locked when I tried it. I pushed it open and walked in, slipping on a pair of gloves before going into the office and work area. That too was empty. I ran to Brewer's office, retrieved the bug, and ran out.

Down the stairs I went, pocketing my gloves, and ran out the door that led to the back of the building.

There were a couple dozen people milling around. One called out, asking if anyone else was in the building. I yelled back I didn't think so and made my way around to the front of the building where the parking lot was.

My car was in the fourth row back from the front door. I took my time getting to it and got in just as the first fire truck arrived. A second and then a third truck arrived. I started the car and drove home. Mission accomplished.

The remainder of the morning, into the afternoon, I worked on typing up the report to Brewer. Per Tina's orders, I left out nothing. I was on the last page, when the doorbell rang. Bea was at her desk and I kept tapping the keys on the keyboard.

In a moment, she entered the Inner Sanctum and closed the door. Tina looked up from her book and I stopped typing.

"Cal's here," she said.

"What does he want?" Tina's tone of voice clearly indicated she was not a happy camper.

"Police business. He says he needs to talk to you."

"Did you set this up, Bea?"

"No, Tina. Honest."

"Why the hell can't he leave me alone?" She had that turn

Medusa to stone look on her face. However, after a quarter minute passed, she sighed, and leaned back in her chair. "Send him in."

Bea went back out to the waiting area and in a moment Cal entered. He headed for the oxblood wingback, thought better of it, and detoured to the chesterfield.

Before he could open his mouth, Tina sat up in her chair and opened hers. "What I want to know, Swenson, is what part of I-don't-want-to-see-you don't you understand?"

"I'm not here to talk about us. If you want to talk about us, we'll have to do that on our own time."

"Over my dead body. There's no *us* to talk about. So what is your excuse this time to weasel your way into my home? Not for one minute do I believe you're here on legitimate police business."

A big smile broke out on his face. "You're wrong, Wright. I *am* here on legitimate and official police business."

The Medusa to stone look re-appeared on Tina's face. "Let's have it. I don't want you here longer than is necessary. We're not friends, Cal Swenson. Do you understand?"

Cal ignored her digs and plowed on. I give him credit for that. A lot of credit. "Congresswoman Horstman is burning up the phones of the Mayor, the County Commissioners, the Chief of Police, the County Sheriff, and for all I know God and even the President. My boss is chewing my ass to get this case wrapped up. I told him about your investigation and that your help would go a long way toward us clearing this up. He took it to the Deputy Chief of Investigations and got approval. The only thing is you only get a thousand bucks special consultant fee. That's it."

"And I suppose I have to work with you."

"Yes."

"What a sweet deal for you, Swenson. I'm—"

I cut her off. "The enemy of my enemy is my friend."

Tina shot daggers in my direction. "What the hell does that mean, Harry?"

"With my own ears I heard you say you were going to kill

whoever shot you with your bare hands. This deal will save you from going to jail."

She leaned back in her chair and closed her eyes. She took in four deep breaths and exhaled them. Her breathing back to normal, she opened her eyes.

Cal said nothing. He just sat on the sofa and looked at her.

She leaned forward and steepled her fingers. "Very well, Swenson. We both want this bastard caught. I'll help you."

"Thanks, Tina. I appreciate it. I'll send over what we have and what we got from the Sheriff's department on the Fishman murder."

He stood, gave a nod of farewell in my direction, and left.

When he was gone, I turned towards the boss. "Why are you so angry, Sis? The guy has been nothing but civil towards you."

"Shut up, Harry."

I have to give Cal a lot of credit. He played Tina like an angler plays a trout. She put up a fight but he reeled her in. If she truly hated him, she would have kicked my comment to the curb. That she didn't, gives me hope they'll be back together. Hopefully sooner, rather than later.

26

THINKING

Wednesday. October 8th

CAL'S PARTNER, SERGEANT KEVIN ROBERTS, WAS ON OUR DOORSTEP at ten to deliver the information the police and sheriff departments had collected. Tina spent the balance of the morning reading through the papers and looking at the photos.

Right after breakfast I'd driven down to the post office on East 31st Street to mail the detailed investigation report to Alex Brewer. Quite a bit further to drive then going downtown, but in my opinion the longer drive was better than fighting traffic and hunting for a parking spot.

I arrived back home a little before Roberts showed up and emailed a summary of the report to Brewer, with an explanation that the full report was in the mail. After he departed, I started looking through the information as Tina passed it over to me. What became obvious, at least to these eyes, was that neither the Sheriff nor the Minneapolis police had a chief suspect in mind. Both agreed the campaign seemed to be the focal point. Beyond that, they were at sea.

"It boils down to motive, doesn't it?" I said.

"Yes." Tina didn't bother looking up from whatever it was she was looking at.

"So who'd want Fishman dead?"

"That we know about? The Congresswoman and Brewer."

"Who'd want Rossiter dead?"

Tina looked up from the piece of paper. "Yes, Harry, the Congresswoman and Brewer are the most reasonable suspects. Both have alibis. Therefore, either the alibis are false or someone who's motive we haven't uncovered did it."

"Okay. Glad my reasoning is still intact. I'm going to make lunch."

I left the office, gave Bea a smooch as I passed, and went on into the kitchen. I decided on oven baked pork chops and sauerkraut, with a lettuce salad.

My mind skimmed over what I knew about the alibis. Madelyn Horstman was at home with her children when Fishman met his end. Pretty sound alibi. It is, though, within the realm of possibility she hired someone to do the deed. The same alibi was given when Rossiter died, with the addition that her husband was also home. Her alibi for the attack on her husband was that she was with a group of big donors having drinks at a bar in downtown Minneapolis. While her alibis appeared sound, they didn't rule out her hiring somebody to do the deeds.

Brewer's alibis were much thinner. Her wife, or hife, as Tina would call her, Abba, was it. To my mind, that seemed pretty thin. If true, Brewer and Abba were together and Brewer didn't actually pull the trigger. Although it didn't mean Brewer couldn't have hired a trigger puller. If the alibis were a lie, then we'd have to get one of the two to crack and I didn't see Brewer cracking.

When lunch was ready, I called the ladies to come and get it. I poured glasses of a German Riesling for Tina and I and water for Bea. We talked about politics, not the Horstman campaign, that's business, but the general tenor of the country and who would win. After our lunch, I suppose one could call it dinner, Bea cleaned up the dishes and put away the leftovers while Tina and I returned to the office. I bounced my ruminations off of her and she agreed they made sense.

"So what are we going to do?"

"Finish looking over the evidence."

I shrugged. "Okay. You're the boss."

We spent the remainder of the afternoon reading through statements and looking at the evidence.

The only thing tying Fishman solidly to the others, aside from the campaign connection, were the two twenty-five caliber bullets in his heart, fired from a pistol pressed to his chest. Up close and personal. His chest would also do a very good job muffling the sound.

Fingerprints were found other than Fishman's, but they didn't lead anywhere. The owners of the prints had either solid alibis or no motive. There were several prints that couldn't be traced.

The information on the Rossiter murder and the shootings at the bar didn't add much to what we already knew. What all this kept coming back to was motive. Who wanted Fishman, Rossiter, Ted Horstman, and Prisca Thoraldson dead? I asked Tina.

She turned her gaze from the picture she was looking at to me. "Horstman's the problem. His death was either a case of being at the wrong place at the wrong time, making Thoraldson the real target, or he was an intended target. If he was an intended target, the question begs to be asked, was his death for purely political reasons?"

"That's what I keep coming to."

"Good, Harry. You're improving."

"Thanks for the complement."

"You're welcome."

"So what do we do, Sis?"

"I don't know. I'm thinking."

"Okay. I'll let you think."

I had some thinking to do as well. Mine was relatively simple. Figuring out what to feed the Great Detective for supper.

After supper, which was leftover roast beef with Madeira Sauce, buttered noodles, and rutabaga, we retired to the living room for tea and Poor Knights of Windsor for dessert. A fire was going in the fireplace and conversation was at a minimum. I suppose we were just enjoying the moment.

Suddenly there were three bangs on the sliding glass doors, which lead out to the deck facing the side yard. All three of us turned and saw a figure silhouetted by the street lights turn and jump off the deck and run off towards the street.

I ran to the doors, crouched down so as not to make an inviting target, opened them, and moved out on to the deck. I peered over the railing and shrubs and surveyed the street. No one in sight. I returned to the living room, closed the doors, and drew the drapes.

"See anything, Harry?"

"No, Sis. Whoever it was must've had wings."

Bea's hand went to her throat, where she still has a scar from flying glass generated by a drive-by shooting of our place back in February. "Wow, Tina, that transparent aluminum really works. Those were bullets, right, Harry?"

"They were, Babe."

After the drive-by, Tina had Bea arrange for the window glass to be replaced with transparent aluminum, which is actually a see-through ceramic. Very expensive stuff. I'm glad she insisted on it.

Tina's lips were pursed. She unpursed them and spoke. "It seems someone doesn't want us working on this case. The question is, what do we know or what does the person think we know that we now pose a threat?"

Somewhere, in the pile of info we have, is the answer. We just have to recognize it for what it is before our luck runs out.

PERSONAE NON GRATAE

Thursday. October 9th

I CALLED AND REPORTED THE SHOOTING TO CAL LAST NIGHT AFTER I was satisfied the shooter hadn't decided to linger. He sent Sergeant Roberts over to take our statements. This morning, after breakfast, he came over himself to take a look at the sliding glass doors.

"This stuff is incredible, Major." He touched the "glass" and fingered the marks the bullets had left.

"This stuff can stop a fifty caliber rifle round hitting it at muzzle velocity."

He whistled. "Is that so? Expensive as hell, I'm guessing."

"Yep. Bea paid for it. Twelve bucks a square inch."

Cal's eyebrows went up. "How many floors, may I ask?"

"First and second."

"My God."

"Yep. Put a dent in her nest egg. But when one almost bleeds to death due to a cut by flying glass…"

"Yeah, puts a different spin on things. You're obviously okay. Tina and Bea?"

"They're fine. Sounded like small rocks hitting the window."

"Transparent aluminum." He shook his head. "Science fiction becomes reality every day."

"That it does."

"Uh, Harry, on a different note, does Tina really hate me?"

I thought a moment before answering. "I think she wants to hate you. I'm not convinced she does. She's feeling hurt and betrayed."

"I know. I really screwed up."

"Personally, I think she loves you and that's why you are seeing this reaction. It's just going to take awhile for her to get over the hurt and betrayal she's feeling."

"Hope I live long enough."

"There is that to consider. She has a memory like an elephant."

"Don't I know it. Well, I'll be seeing you around, Major."

"Bye, Cal."

I went inside and he took off to wherever he needed to be. Bea was at her desk and Tina, according to Bea and my ears, was taking a half-hour break to play the piano. From the sound of the music, my guess was our friend Chopin was getting a workout. I sat at my desk and looked over the police information. I'd made copies so Tina and I no longer had to share.

Now we could add Tina, and perhaps Bea and myself, to the list of intended victims. And what was the connection? The Horstman campaign is all I could see. And why kill us? What did we know that made us a danger? I had no idea.

Tina hobbled in using her cane for support and sat at her desk. Before I had a chance to say anything, she held up her hand. "I know you were going to start badgering me. Don't. I want to talk to the Congresswoman, Brewer, and Brewer's hife. Separately. As soon as possible."

I turned to the phone, dialed a number, and got Opal, the receptionist. The thought momentarily occurred to me that maybe she never sleeps.

"Hello, Mr. Wright, how may I help you?"

"My boss, Justinia Wright, requests a meeting with Madelyn Horstman at her earliest convenience."

"I'm afraid that's not possible, Mr. Wright. Alex Brewer—"

I cut her off. "We are special consultants to the Minneapolis Police Department. Tell Alex Brewer she can either cooperate with us or we'll have the police take the Congresswoman down to headquarters and we'll talk to her there."

No sound came from the other end. Finally, "All right, Mr. Wright, I'll put you though to Vi Nguyen. She's handling the Congresswoman's schedule. Hold please."

I held and in a few seconds Vi's voice was greeting me.

"Hi, Vi. Justinia Wright would like a meeting with Ms. Horstman as soon as possible at our place in Minneapolis."

"Not possible, Harry. You and Ms. Wright are *persona non grata*. Per Alex Brewer's order."

"Actually it's *personae non gratae*."

"What?"

"Plural. *Persona non grata* is singular."

"Oh."

"But back to your point, sorry to inform you we're working with the Minneapolis Police Department as special consultants. This is police business, Vi."

"I see. Well, I don't know. The—"

"Vi, I can have Lieutenant Cal Swenson from Minneapolis Homicide arrest the lot of you for obstructing the course of an official police investigation. I don't think you want that."

"You wouldn't."

"Oh, yes, I would. Alex Brewer hasn't been the most pleasant person to work with. I'd love to see her show up in handcuffs."

"You're not being very nice."

"Since when did you become an Alex Brewer fan."

"Well, I'm… I'll call you back in a couple minutes."

"Okay." I gave her the office number and hung up.

Without looking up from whatever it was she was looking at, Tina said, "Problems?"

"Seems Brewer has finally gotten her way. We're *personae non gratae.*"

"Doesn't mean a thing. As you pointed out, we're with the police."

"I think that's thrown them for a loop."

The phone rang and I answered it. "Wright Investigations."

"Harry, Vi Nguyen. Mad won't meet with your boss alone. She insists Alex be there too."

"No dice. I guess she'll be coming here on the arm of a man in blue who's pledged to serve and protect. And I wouldn't be surprised if it was at a time most inconvenient for the Congresswoman. The police have a difficult job, not that I'm a rabid fan of the police, mind you. But as I said, they have a difficult job and when a politician tries to make their job more difficult by trying to get the legislation passed that the Congresswoman sponsored, well, I wouldn't be surprised if they'd pick her up at a time that might cause her some embarrassment. Maybe a speech or something."

"Harry, that's blackmail."

"Technically, no, it isn't. You should know that, Vi. You're a lawyer. I was merely presenting a hypothetical scenario based on human nature."

"Call it what you want, Harry, the effect is the same."

"The choice is the Congresswoman's, Vi. Now, since you folks have decided you want to obstruct an official police investigation, Ms. Horstman can be here at Miss Wright's office tomorrow at one pm sharp. If she's not here, alone, someone very official will be sent out to escort her here."

"I thought you were a nice person, Harry. But you're not. You're mean and nasty. And the Congresswoman has friends and her friends can put you out of a job."

"Now who's being mean and nasty? I'm investigating a murder. You can play games and threaten all you want. But with the evidence we have, Ms. Horstman just might not see the inside of the Capitol building after January unless she's a tourist. So tomorrow. At one. Bye, Vi." And I hung up the phone.

Tina was looking at me. "Getting married was good for you, Harry. Now you don't let these young women get to you anymore. Glad I got you and Bea together."

"Now wait one minute. I was not a pushover."

"Were too."

"Was not."

"Were too."

"Good grief. I was not. Now what about Brewer? Should I have Cal get her?"

"Were too and, yes, it will probably be easier."

"And Abba?"

"Why don't you try calling her? She might be more willing to pay us a visit."

I looked through the paperwork, found Brewer's home number, and dialed it. A woman's voice answered and I introduced myself. Her accent was not pronounced and her speech was measured and the pace deliberate.

"What can I do for you, Mr. Wright?"

"Wright Investigations is operating as a special consultant to the Minneapolis police in their investigations of the murders of Damon Rossiter and Theodore Horstman. Miss Wright, who was wounded in the attack on Mr. Horstman, would like to ask you a few questions. Would you be able to come to her office to do so?"

"I have already talked to the police. I have nothing more to say."

"Miss Wright and I have read your statement and she has some further questions the police didn't ask."

"I have nothing more to say."

"I see. Very well. We'll have to do this the hard way then."

"What do you mean?"

"We are going to have to have a police officer pick you up and take you to Minneapolis police headquarters downtown and then we'll have to interview you there."

There was a pause. "Very well. I will come tomorrow. What time?"

"Does ten in the morning work for you?"

"That will work, yes. What is your address?"

I gave her the address and the call ended.

"The only reasonable one in the bunch," I said.

"Hopefully she tells us the truth."

"Should I call Cal to round up the Congresswoman or wait and see if she shows up?"

"No. We'll wait and see if she shows up on her own. I'd prefer that."

"Of course, if Brewer and Horstman have anything to hide, they'll be figuring out what line to take."

"I know, Harry. I wasn't born last night."

"Sorry, just making conversation."

"This will be like a chess game. Those two women aren't stupid. However, if they're telling lies, hopefully I'll get them to trip themselves. Play the gambit and hope they lose themselves in the ensuing complications."

"You think they're guilty?"

"Everyone's guilty. Whether or not they committed the murders or hired someone to do so is another question. And one I'm not prepared to answer. Not just yet."

NO SHOW

Friday. October 10th

THE TIME WAS TWO MINUTES AFTER TEN WHEN THE DOORBELL RANG. A couple minutes passed before Bea showed in Abba Muhammad, Alex Brewer's hife. I introduced Tina and myself to her and guided her to the oversized oxblood wingback. She was a tall, slim woman with shoulder length hair. She wore a bit of makeup and was dressed in black slacks and a purple blouse. Her jewelry was gold and tasteful. She sat in the chair, her posture erect.

"I am here, Miss Wright. Ask your questions."

"Do you love Alex Brewer?"

"Yes. She is very good to me. I know she is with other women. But she is good to me."

"Doesn't that bother you? Your spouse being with other partners?"

"Yes, it bothers me. She does not beat me, as my husband did. She is kind to me and gentle. One day, she'll be too old and women will no longer find her attractive. Then I will have her all to myself. When sex will no longer matter and only companionship will be important. She is in her heart of hearts a good person."

"You have provided alibis for each other for the murders of Damon Rossiter, Simon Fishman, and Theodore Horstman. Did you lie about any of them?"

"If I did, do you think I'd tell you? I am Alex Brewer's wife. My duty is to her. To protect her, cherish her, love her. I will die before I will betray her."

"Ms. Brewer maintains a busy schedule. Am I right to assume you are home alone much of the time?"

"I am alone often. I am also at the Somali youth center. I volunteer my time."

"How often are you there."

"Four or five times a week."

"What time of day?"

"Mostly afternoons. Sometimes evenings."

"Would you like children, Ms. Muhammad?"

"Yes. Alex has promised we'll try to get a baby when the campaign is over."

"Adopt?"

"We might do that. We might try in vitro fertilization. We haven't decided."

"Because of spousal privilege, you don't have to disclose information that passes between you and Alex, should there be a trial, nor do you have to testify against her. So between you and me, did you lie when you provided alibis for Alex?"

Abba smiled and it was a pretty smile. "My duty, Miss Wright, is to protect my marriage partner. I will not betray her. She was with me those nights of the murders. That is what I told the police and that is what I am telling you."

Tina leaned back in her chair. "That's your story and you're sticking to it."

"Yes."

"Does your spouse know you're here?"

"No. She would not want me to be here."

"Thank you for your time, Ms. Muhammad."

Abba stood. "Alex is a good person at heart."

"If you say so, Ms. Muhammad."

"I do." Abba turned and walked to the door, where I was waiting to open it for her. Bea did the honors of escorting her to the front door and out into the crisp October weather.

Back in the Inner Sanctum, I returned to my desk.

"Well, Sis, you didn't get too far with her."

"On the contrary, Harry, I got quite a bit from Ms. Muhammad. Quite a bit."

"If you say so. Do you think the Congresswoman's going to show up?"

"I don't know. Depends how stubborn Brewer wants to be. Did Cal say when he might bring her to us?"

I'd called Cal yesterday afternoon to let him know Tina wanted to interview Brewer. "He said he'd bring her over as soon as possible."

"Go make lunch. Bea is watching the phone and door. Let's eat at noon. Just in case she does show up."

"Okay, Boss."

I left the office, giving Bea a smooch on my way to the kitchen.

For supper I was planning on a pork roast with sauerkraut, potatoes, Brussels sprouts, and an apple pie. For lunch, I thought a beef pot pie would taste good. I had left over roast beef to use up. I was going to be just a wee bit on the busy side. Personally, my money was on Mad Horstman not showing up. With her husband dead, the Congresswoman had ceded control of her life over to Brewer. We were now the enemy.

Noon rolled around and the pot pie was ready. I uncorked a bottle of Northern Vineyards St. Croix. A luscious, earthy, smoky, peppery wine. Personally, I prefer Leon Millot. However, the grape seems to have lost out to Marechal Foch and Minnesota-bred grapes. I know Leon Millot and Marechal Foch are supposed to be genetic twins. My palate prefers Millot to Foch. Anyway, St. Croix makes good wine. I won't complain too loudly. I called the ladies and we filled up on pot pie and ice cream.

Tina and I were back at our posts by five before one. Bea had cleanup duties. But one o'clock came and went and when the clock told me the time was half-past one, I made a call to Cal and asked him to add Madelyn Horstman to the list of folks Tina would like to talk to. He said he'd get her to us ASAP and I passed the info on to Tina.

"Harry, call David, Gwen, and Ed. I want David and Gwen to tail Brewer and you and Ed to tail Horstman. Start as soon as possible."

"Will do." I got on the phone and got all three. David and Gwen were available immediately. Ed said he could start tomorrow afternoon. I relayed the information to Tina.

"Good. Harry, I'd like you to start now. If you can get her alone, try to talk to her."

"Okay, Boss. I'm on it."

I told Bea what supper was and she said she'd take care of it. I told her I'd see her when I saw her and was out the door.

Just in case I had occasion to use it, I put one of the drones in the trunk and took off for the Horstman residence.

On the way there, I called Bea and asked her to call the Horstman campaign and find out where the Congresswoman was. I told her to pretend she was a newspaper reporter.

In a few minutes she called back and told me the Congress-woman was speaking at a women's auxiliary in Shorewood at three and after that at a dinner in Loretto at seven. I thanked her and redirected the car to the southwest corner of the metro area. With a little bit of luck I might just make it in time.

29

TAKING ONE FOR THE TEAM

Friday Afternoon. October 10th

I WAS AT THE SHOREWOOD CITY OFFICE BUILDING AT TEN AFTER THREE. The women's auxiliary was meeting in one of the community rooms. The building was a typical nondescript one story office building. I walked in, found the meeting, and was denied entrance because I wasn't a member or guest of a member.

The person watching the door also didn't give two hoots that I was a special consultant to the Minneapolis Police Department. Her words were, "Does this look like Minneapolis?" I had to agree with her it didn't and that was that. So I waited.

At eight after four, people started leaving the room. I walked over to the door and opened it. The door monitor was still there.

"Meeting's over," I said. "May I enter?"

"Do you have a meeting in here?"

"Yes," I told her, although her face had a *you're lying* look on it. I didn't care what she thought because I saw Susan Wikstrom and Alex Brewer, along with Madelyn Horstman.

Out came my phone, I told it to call "Cal", and, when he answered, told him I was looking at our quarry and where we all were. He thanked me and hung up. I walked over to the

Congresswoman, who was talking to a woman. Alex Brewer almost ran to put herself physically between Horstman and me.

"You are not welcome," she hissed.

"And you are going to jail for obstructing an official investigation. If you want, I'll visit."

"I'd rather see you dead, first."

"I'd be careful what you say. Somebody might hear you and think you were serious, even though I know you were only speaking metaphorically."

"Get out."

"No. This is a public building. We the public own it."

"You don't live in this city."

"Neither do you. So maybe neither of us should be here."

"We were invited. You weren't."

"I'm on police business. I think that's an automatic invitation."

"You aren't talking to Mad."

"Okay. I'll talk to you, instead."

"You aren't talking to me either."

"Well if you aren't talking, who is? I see your mouth moving."

"You are a piece of work."

"Why, thank you. You aren't so bad yourself, actually. So, since we are agreed, how about we go over to that corner and talk."

I was a little slow. I did move enough that her fist only gave me a glancing blow. Seeing my chance, I played it for all it was worth and fell on the floor, clutching my face, moaning, and groaning.

From somewhere, I heard, "Oh my God! She hit him!"

That was music to my ears. A witness. Slowly, I got to my feet. Brewer was looking at me, fists clenched. I looked around. "Who saw her hit me?"

A woman, pushing seventy, called out, "I did."

"Thank you, ma'am. May I have your name and phone number?"

She gave me both. Out came my cell and I called 911. When

the call was answered, I made my report. When finished, I turned to Brewer.

"You are in a wee bit of trouble, Lassie." And doggone if she didn't plug me again. I guess it was a case of in for a penny, in for a pound. She connected, too. I saw stars and ended up on the floor. Nothing like taking one for the team.

It didn't take long for a cop to show up. He questioned Brewer, me, and Mrs. Holm, the woman who was the witness. I told the officer I wanted to press charges and he took Alex Brewer away with him.

Just after Brewer left, Cal showed up.

"You're going to have one hell of a bruise, Major."

"Worth it, Cal. Brewer was arrested for assault."

"She hit you?"

"Yep. Didn't like my suggestion we find a corner and talk."

He started laughing.

I had my hands on my hips. "What's so funny?"

"You, Harry. Okay. So we know where one of Tina's suspects is. Where's the other one?"

I looked around. "Ah, crap." Wikstrom and Horstman were gone. "Horstman and her field director must've left while Brewer was using me for a punching bag. But I do know where Horstman's supposed to be at seven."

"Spill the beans."

I gave him the address.

"Okay, Major. I'll retrieve Brewer and have Roberts pick up Horstman. You go home and get some ice on your face."

We walked out to our cars. "Any idea where Tina's going with this?"

"Nope. She's keeping her cards close to her chest."

He nodded, paused, and then said, "Okay. See you later."

On the way home, I thought about the fireworks that were going to begin in short order. Probably make the M80s and cherry bombs I played with when a kid sound like party poppers.

30

THE QUESTIONS BEGIN

Friday Night. October 10th

By the time I got home, Bea and Tina had finished eating supper. They were having pie and tea in the living room.

When Bea saw me, she blurted out, "Harry! You're hurt!" She hugged me, said she'd get ice, and went to the kitchen.

"Alex Brewer hit me. Twice. There was a witness and I called 911. Cal's going to bring Brewer to us as soon as he can. Fifth degree assault, I should imagine. Cause her a bit of grief. The campaign too, come to think of it."

Tina shook her head and started laughing. "Your target was Horstman."

"Yeah. Got confused in the heat of the battle. Anyway, Cal's partner, Roberts, is going to bring in Horstman. So I guess we can call off the gang."

"I suppose so."

Bea was back with the ice pack. I applied it to my face and asked her to call David, Gwen, and Ed to tell them they were on hold for the time being.

"Hungry?"

Tina was asking me if I was hungry? Huh. That's a new one. I told her I was and she and Bea got up and went to the kitchen. Bea returned with a glass of wine and Tina came back with a plate of food.

"Thank you, my wonderful ladies."

Bea held the ice pack to my face so I'd have my hands free to eat. The supper was very good, Bea's a good cook. And when the last morsel was gone, we moved to the office. Bea retrieved her tatting on the way. Once we were seated in our usual spots, I reported on the afternoon's excitement.

Bea laughed. "You really fell down and pretended you were hurt?"

"Sure," I replied. "Had to make it look good to draw attention."

"And it worked," Tina said. "Good work, Big Brother. I'm proud of you."

"Gee thanks, Sis. Always glad to take one for the team, as they say. So now what?"

"I'll see when they get here. Probably take Brewer a few hours to get bail. Therefore we might see Horstman first. In any case, I'll have to play it by ear."

"Do you even know what you're looking for?" I asked.

"Not really. In this case, though, all roads lead back to the campaign and Brewer runs the campaign. Horstman may or may not be in the know. I have a hunch Brewer knows more about this than she's saying. However, it's just a hunch. I could be completely off base."

The phone rang. I looked at the clock on my desk. Twenty after eight. "Wright Investigations."

"Mr. Wright? This is Sergeant Kevin Roberts. I have Madelyn Horstman and we are on our way."

"Thanks, Kevin. See you when you get here." I hung up the phone and turned to Tina. "Horstman's on her way."

"Thanks." She lit a cigar and poured a glass of madeira. After taking a sip of wine, she puffed on her cigar, sent a cloud of smoke to the ceiling, leaned back in her chair, and closed her eyes.

Now we waited.

————

The doorbell rang a little after nine. I went to the door and let in Sergeant Roberts and Madelyn Horstman. The look on the Congresswoman's face showed she wasn't a happy camper.

"I'm going to make your life very difficult," Horstman said from between clenched teeth.

"I'm just the help," I replied. "Save the good stuff for the boss." To Roberts, I said, "This way."

Into the Inner Sanctum I led them. Roberts took a position by the door and I indicated Horstman should take the oxblood oversized wingback, which she did. She looked small sitting in it.

"You are going to pay for this harassment, Miss Wright."

Tina folded her arms on her desk. "Figuratively or actually?"

The Congresswoman looked at her. "I hope both. My husband is dead, my campaign in ruins, my best friend in jail. I can't even grieve for him. I hate you. I paid you to help me and you screwed me over."

"Mrs. Horstman, you can blame whoever you want. However, the reality remains, whether you want to accept it or not, that your best friend had your campaign in a shambles before you hired me. The reality also is that to get back at your best friend someone betrayed you."

"Well, that person is gone. Alex has assured me the person was dealt with."

Tina sat up straight. "By whom?"

"Whoever is doing the killings. The person who betrayed me was Prisca Thoraldson. And she is no longer part of my campaign."

"And how do you know this? That she was passing on information?"

"Alex got information and we were going to let her go after securing the donor list, but then Prisca was wounded when—"

The Congresswoman started sobbing. I got up and made sure she had a box of tissues by her side. She didn't bother to thank me.

Tina interrupted the crying. "Apparently you haven't heard."

Horstman looked up. "Heard what?"

"We told Vi Nguyen we had evidence of who was giving information to your opponents. We just weren't ready to act on it, but would have been in just a few more days."

"You're lying."

"Mrs. Horstman, everyone lies. On this, however, I'm not lying. I do have the evidence."

"I want to see it."

"Talk to your best friend, your campaign manager."

"Alex has it?"

"Yes. Didn't she share it with you?"

"No."

"We emailed a summary and mailed a physical copy of the full report. Harry?"

"I have the receipt right here, Mrs. Horstman. Mailed it myself. Ms. Brewer should have gotten it the following day."

"When was this?" Madelyn asked.

I checked my calendar. "She should've gotten it yesterday."

"She didn't say anything to me. I want to see the report."

"No." Tina's voice was stern. "You're here on a matter far more important than political espionage. You're here so we can talk about murder."

"I killed no one. I don't believe in guns. They should be outlawed. The ammunition too. Surely, you don't think I did these killings. My own husband?"

"I don't think. I deduce. And, yes, it's possible you killed your husband either directly or indirectly because it has been known for one spouse to kill their better or worse half."

"I don't even own a gun. So I couldn't have done it."

"You could have hired someone or borrowed the gun or someone could have done you a favor."

"Well, I didn't and no one did me any *favors*."

"Very well, your statement is noted. Now, please tell me where you were the night of Friday, the twenty-sixth of September between the hours of ten and midnight."

"I've already given this to the police."

From the back of the room came Roberts's voice. "Miss Wright is working for the police and wants to ask you again. Please answer the question."

"I think I want my attorney here."

"Very well," Tina said, "call your attorney."

Horstman took out her phone and made a call. In a moment she said, "John, I'm being questioned again by the police. Actually someone working for the police. I'd like you to be here." A pause. "No. I'm at the home of Justinia Wright, who's— Oh, you've heard of her. Okay. Do you know the address? No? Just a minute."

I furnished the Congresswoman with our address, which she passed on to her lawyer. When she was done with the call, she told us he'd join the party in half an hour.

"Harry, take Mrs. Horstman to one of the spare bedrooms."

The Congresswoman, Roberts, and myself filed out of the office and went upstairs, where I put her in a spare bedroom and Roberts stood guard outside. Being on the second floor, I didn't think we had to worry about her going out a window in an escape attempt. I went back down to the office and sat at my desk.

"She wants her attorney," I said. "Is she guilty?"

"Scared, more likely," Tina replied. "Or just wants to be a pain in the ass."

The doorbell rang. I went to see who it was and saw a woman standing on the porch. I opened the door.

"May I help you?"

"I'm Hester Palmquist. I'm Alex Brewer's attorney."

"I'm Harry Wright. Alex isn't here yet."

"Apparently she's on her way."

"I see. Come in, then."

I put Hester in the waiting room, asked if she wanted tea, the offer of which she declined, and continued on to the Inner Sanctum.

"Brewer's attorney is in the waiting room. Alex is on her way."

Bea quipped, "We're having a party."

"Not sure I'd call it that, Babe."

Bea went on, "We'll make it one. Shall I get refreshments?"

Tina's voice was louder than necessary. "No."

"It would be polite, Sis."

"No. They're not my guests."

The doorbell rang. I trekked back out to the entryway and let in Cal Swenson and Alex Brewer.

"Good evening, Alex," I said. "So good to see you out and about."

She ignored me. "Thank God you're here, Hester, so we can get this farce over with."

Even though I felt slighted at being ignored, I put on a brave face and led everyone into the Inner Sanctum. Bea said she'd wait at her desk in the outer office so she could let in Horstman's lawyer when he showed up. I told her what room the Congress-woman was in.

I sat at my desk. Cal was standing in the back of the room by the door. Tina had already introduced herself to Brewer's attorney and now no one was saying anything. I got out my notebook and my digital recorder. Time to get in more shorthand practice. That is, if anyone decided to speak. Cal did.

"Miss Wright is working with the Minneapolis police depart-ment to help solve the murders of Simon Fishman, Damon Rossiter, Theodore Horstman, and Andrew Foglar, he was the person who tried to stop the attacker at Jimmy's nightclub, as well as the attempted murders of Prisca Thoraldson and Miss Wright. Please answer her questions."

And that's when the doorbell rang.

31

STONEWALLED

Late Friday Night. October 10th

IN A MINUTE, BEA POKED HER HEAD IN AND ANNOUNCED JOHN Penney had arrived, Horstman's attorney. "Should I have him wait out here?"

Tina leaned back in her chair and stayed that way for a good thirty seconds. When she leaned forward, she told Bea to send him in and to get the Congresswoman. We were going to have a party after all.

Penney entered and took a seat on the chesterfield, where Palmquist was sitting. Five minutes later Horstman and Sergeant Roberts joined us. Brewer relinquished the oversized wingback to the Congresswoman and took a seat on the chesterfield with the legal team.

Now Tina had her work cut out for her and she took her time looking over the group. Cal and Roberts were standing in the back of the room, on either side of the door. At last she spoke.

"All this folderol over a few simple questions. I can't help but think these are the actions of guilty people. If you were innocent, why the fuss? There shouldn't be any. Guilty people, on the other hand, obfuscate and complicate and hide behind attorneys."

Palmquist interrupted. "It's late. We didn't come here to get a lecture. Ask your questions, so we can go home."

Tina smiled. "I shall. Don't you worry. I needn't go over recent events in detail. The principals know them. Let me simply say this case has confirmed my belief that politics is a dirty business, a very dirty business. Now, then, Mrs. Horstman, let's start with you. Simon Fishman had information which you feared he'd make public. Or possibly use to blackmail you. Is that correct?"

"Yes, that's correct."

"That constitutes motive. The motive of elimination. Eliminate the threat and you breathe easier."

"But I was at home with my children the night he died. Ted came home later."

"How old are your children, Mrs. Horstman?"

"Donna's nine and Teddy's six."

"They're awfully young."

"Janet, the girl next door who was babysitting, can verify when I arrived home. She's sixteen."

"Miss Wright, just where are you going with this?" Penney asked.

"I'm trying to get a feel for how strong Mrs. Horstman's alibi is. She has motive. Did she have means and opportunity as well?"

Penney nodded his head and leaned back on the sofa.

"Ms. Brewer, your only alibi is that of your hife. Is that correct?"

"My *wife* is my alibi, yes. She should be sufficient. She's an adult."

"But hardly unbiased. Practically speaking, it proves nothing and you know it. She can't be compelled to testify against you."

Brewer said nothing and just smiled.

Tina continued. "The same can be said, Ms. Brewer, for the murders of Damon Rossiter and Theodore Horstman. You also have motive. That of elimination. Get rid of the threat to the person and career of the woman you love."

Madelyn Horstman, in a very loud voice, said, "Alex wouldn't kill Ted. She wouldn't deprive me of my husband or my children of their father."

Tina fixed the Congresswoman with a stern gaze. "How naive can you be? If she loved you enough, she could very well do such a thing."

Madelyn seemed to wilt. Her voice was soft. "No. No, she wouldn't."

Palmquist interrupted. "Ms. Brewer has an alibi which means even if she had a motive, she didn't have opportunity."

"As long as the alibi holds, Ms. Palmquist."

Palmquist smiled. "I don't think you'll budge Abba, if — and that is a big if — she's lying."

"So I'm told," Tina said and turned her attention to Cal. "Lieutenant Swenson, the Horstman children were not interviewed apart from parental presence, were they?"

"No. They weren't."

"Mrs. Horstman, why did you pursue a career in Congress when your husband was opposed to it?"

"Because I felt it important."

"More important than your marriage?"

"He didn't stop me."

"No, he didn't. But he very clearly did not want you in Washington and was fairly vocal about it. Didn't you think about how your absence would affect your children and your marriage?"

"Miss Wright, where are you going with this?" John Penney asked.

"Mr. Penney, I'm trying to understand the drivers in this case. I'm not married. However, if I was I certainly don't think I'd want to do something contrary to the desires of the man I loved. I'd at least want to work out a win-win compromise."

Penney waved his hand to indicate Tina could continue.

Tina turned her attention back to the Congresswoman. "So, Mrs. Horstman, why was your career more important than your marriage?"

"What makes you say that, Miss Wright?"

"You in Washington, facing the numerous temptations that are there. Your husband, alone, here."

"My marriage was fine, Miss Wright."

"Was it? Harry, what did Mr. Horstman say to you?"

"Just a minute." I paged through my notes until I found the ones I'd made of our conversation in the restaurant. "Here it is. I have it pretty much verbatim.

"I asked, 'What's your role in your wife's campaign?'

"He replied, 'Don't really have one. Mostly I just stand by her side and smile.'

"Me: 'What about when she is in Washington?'

"Mr. Horstman: 'Look, Harry, I have a business to run. This politics stuff is Maddie's. I'd rather she was here in Minnesota. I don't like her being in Washington. Not a good crowd there.'

"Me: 'So why do you let her? Or do you?'

"Mr. Horstman: 'This is something Maddie really wants. No use trying to stop her. It's like hitting your head against a wall. It feels good when you stop. I stopped. Get my drift?'

"Me: 'I do. So you don't interfere with her political ambitions and you have peace.'

"Mr. Horstman: 'That about says it all.'

"Me: 'Have kids?'

"He nodded his head to indicate he did.

"I asked, 'So you run the business and take care of the kids and she helps run the country.'

"He replied, 'You got it.'

"That was what Mr. Horstman said to me on Thursday, September 25th."

"Thank you, Harry." Tina turned her attention to Alex. "Ms. Brewer, I suppose you liked the situation."

"What do you mean?"

"Having Mrs. Horstman all to yourself in Washington."

"My relationship to Mad has nothing to do with these murders."

"Au contraire. It has everything to do with them. Why did you not share the report we sent you with Mrs. Horstman?"

"I haven't received it."

Tina turned to me. "Harry?"

I looked at my notes. "The post office has recorded our envelope was received."

"So, Ms. Brewer, why did you keep it secret from Mrs. Horstman. Who just so happens to be your boss and friend?"

Palmquist tried to run interference. "What has this—"

"Shut up, Ms. Palmquist. Your interruptions are dragging this out and *you* were the one bellyaching about going home."

Madelyn jumped into the fray. "Alex, if you got the report from Miss Wright why didn't you at least tell me about it?"

Now all eyes were on Alex Brewer. She licked her lips.

Tina fanned the fire. "Yes, Ms. Brewer, why didn't you share the information? Surely, you stood to gain from it. What did you stand to lose?"

Palmquist decided to play the part of the cavalry coming over the hill. "Don't answer, Alex. This has nothing to do with anything."

Tina didn't give up. "It has everything to do with everything. Very well, Mrs. Horstman, I'll summarize the information for you because your dysfunctional campaign is not working for your best interests. I and my team discovered there were two spies in your campaign. The first one began selling you out during the primary and as you surmised that person was Prisca Thoraldson. However, she didn't pass the information on to Fishman or, later, Aagard. No, that job was done by your husband."

"You're lying. Ted would never betray me."

"On the contrary, Mrs. Horstman. He did. Twice. He not only gave away campaign secrets, thereby betraying your dream of a political career, he was having an affair with Ms. Thoraldson and thereby also betraying his marital commitment to you."

Horstman jumped up. "You're lying. You have no proof."

"You want proof?"

Penney spoke. "Maybe you don't want to see the proof, Madelyn. If Miss Wright says she has proof, she probably does. Her reputation is almost legendary."

Horstman slowly sank back onto the chair, muttering, "No. It can't be."

The look on Brewer's face was as hateful a look as I think I've ever seen. Not even my ex could match it.

Tina damned the torpedoes and went full steam ahead. "Damon Rossiter was a spy for Aagard. When you won the primary, your husband, bound and determined to get you out of Washington, contacted Aagard's campaign and began passing on the information Ms. Thoraldson gathered for him. Rossiter, in turn, passed on false information, primarily by doing Jawanda Clark's research for her. Spies, traitors, and laziness, coupled with a despised campaign manager are what have torpedoed your campaign, Mrs. Horstman."

The Congresswoman's face was blank.

"Of course, as I have already said, campaign espionage is minor compared to murder. The question before us, Ms. Brewer and Mrs. Horstman, is how much do you know about the murders and how involved were you in their prosecution. Would you like to tell me?"

I'm not sure Madelyn Horstman even heard what Tina said. She seemed preoccupied with all of the betrayal. Brewer, on the other hand, heard every word and came to her friend's rescue.

"Neither of us had anything to do with any of the murders. You have our alibis. Even if we had motive, neither of us had opportunity. You are stymied, Miss Wright."

Tina leaned back in her chair, folded her arms, and closed her eyes. I looked at the clock. The time was heading towards midnight. She sat up. "Very well. Since you want to do this the hard way, we are finished for tonight."

Penney said he'd take Madelyn home and Palmquist volunteered to do the same for Brewer. Both accepted.

"I'd like to talk to Lieutenant Swenson and Sergeant Roberts," Tina said.

Bea saw Horstman, Brewer, and the lawyers out. I stayed to see what my sister had to say to our police friends.

"Lieutenant Swenson, does Brewer or Horstman own a gun?"

"Nothing on record."

"You may want to search their residences, vehicles, and offices. Although I doubt you'll find the weapon."

"So they're the ones?"

"Yes. But they're clever. Well, Brewer, actually. We are going to have to trip her up. How, is the question."

"All right, Miss Wright, we'll do the searches and see what we come up with," Cal said.

"Very good. Goodnight."

Cal and Roberts left. Bea joined us after closing and locking the front door.

"What do we do now, Sis?"

"It won't be admissible in court, but it may help us find the weak link in the chain. Call Gwen. I want her to hack Horstman's and Brewer's smartphones. We'll start there."

I was wondering when Tina was going to resort to Gwen's hacking expertise. A Universal Data Extraction Device is the nemesis of every privacy loving American. Police departments use them to snoop on us. You roll through a stop sign and are stopped by those dedicated to serve and protect. He or she can zap your phone and get all of your data before stepping out of the squad car. Even the password protected stuff. Welcome to 1984. Big Brother *is* watching you.

32

THE STRONG MAN IS STRONGEST ALONE

Saturday. October 11th

RATHER THAN CALL GWEN, DUE TO THE TIME BEING SOMEWHAT AFTER midnight, I texted her. I got a text back at 7:23 this morning letting me know she was on it.

The morning was nothing out of the ordinary for us. I let Buddy out, made sure the cats and dog had food and water, dodged said cats and dog chasing each other, made tea, prepared the victuals, and retrieved the newspaper.

I had just sat down at the table with my tea and the paper when Bea joined me. Tina came down a few minutes later. After the murmur, which I assumed was "Good Morning" and before she stuck her nose in her iPad, I let her know Gwen was in pursuit of our quarry. She replied with an audible, "Good".

After breakfast, Bea went grocery shopping and Tina and I went to the office. When we'd settled in at our respective desks, I asked, "How's your leg?"

"Thank you for asking. It hurts often and sometimes I wonder if I'll ever be able to walk normally again. Then I tell myself the pain will go away and one day I'll be able to ditch the cane and walk just as well as I ever did."

"So you think it's Brewer."

"Yes."

"Statistically speaking, a firearm is not the weapon of choice for a woman."

"True. Brewer, though, in my opinion, is very masculine. How she thinks, how she competes. I can see her using a firearm."

"So how do we get her to confess?"

"By finding the weakest link in the chain. Finding the one to whom pressure, when applied, will cause her to crack."

"Abba or Madelyn?"

"Or one of the other staffers."

"What's the motive?"

"Elimination. Brewer told us herself she's in love with Madelyn Horstman. Would marry her if she could. Alex Brewer was eliminating the threats to the one person she loves and cares the most about. Now, we have to find the weak link and get that person to crack and spill the beans."

"Saw a poll in the paper this morning. Aagard's out in front by fifteen points. I think it's all over for Horstman. Can't wait to see what Brewer's arrest for assault will do to the campaign."

"If Horstman was smart, she'd dump Brewer. But she won't. Truth be told, she cares too much for the woman. Why, is beyond me."

And with that, Tina picked up a book and started reading.

I went about the day as I usually do. Typed up the notes I'd made thus far on the case. Like to keep the paperwork current. Made note of expenses and checked the bank balance. When Bea got back home, I helped her put away the groceries and then made lunch. Today it was hamburgers, which I cooked on the grill.

In the afternoon, I drove out to both Horstman's and Brewer's residences. I talked with Janey Bascomb, a fifty-something woman, who Mad had just hired to watch the children. She was a live-in domestic worker and this was her second day on the job. She was from a small town on the Iron Range, recently widowed, and needed a job. I filed the information away. People need jobs because they need money. Offer them enough money and they might tell you things.

At Brewer's house, I knocked on the door and Abba answered.

"You are Mr. Wright. The detective."

"Yes, I am. Good afternoon."

"Good afternoon. What do you want?"

"Aside from the truth and a winning lottery ticket, not much."

"I have nothing more to say to you."

"I know. I, though, have something to say to you."

"Say it, please."

"If you need a good divorce lawyer, let me know. Now that Mad Horstman has no husband, and given that your spouse confessed to my boss and me her undying love for Mrs. Horstman, well, I'm just saying if you need a good divorce lawyer I know one."

Abba looked at me through narrowed eyes. I plowed on.

"You might want to consider, as well, that continuing to defend Alex is tantamount to having faith in the *Titanic* being unsinkable after it hit the iceberg. Just saying. After all, free advice is free and you get what you pay for. Sometimes, though, you get a bargain. Have a good day."

I turned and left. When I reached my car, I saw Abba watching me and waved to her. She, however, didn't wave back. I had sown a seed. Now we wait to see if it sprouts and gives us fruit. I got into my car and drove home.

Bea was vacuuming. Supper was roast chicken with mashed potatoes and gravy, lima beans in cream, a lettuce salad, and an apple pie for dessert. I started in on the pie, as that would take the longest. The pastry was in the fridge, chilling, and I was peeling and coring apples when the phone rang. I wiped my hands and answered it.

"Wright Investigations."

"Harry, Gwen. I got the information and am going over it now. I'll stop by later tonight."

"Thanks, Gwen. I'll let Tina know. See you."

I hung up the phone, found Tina in the office sitting by the fire reading. I reported, she grunted an acknowledgement, and I returned to the kitchen to finish up the pie and get on with the rest of the supper preparations.

When the chicken was in the oven, Bea, vacuuming finished, took over the remaining supper preparations and I joined Tina in the office. She was listening to Elgar's First Symphony on the sound system.

"At this point, everything seems to be hanging on what Gwen finds."

"We'll see. We aren't out of options, Harry, we may just have to start getting more creative."

The phone rang and I answered it. The voice on the other end was Cal.

"Hey, Major. Just letting you know we came up empty handed on the searches."

"Thanks, Cal. Appreciate the call."

I hung up the phone and before I could say anything, Tina said, "The searches came up with nothing."

"Correct."

"Thought so. Now let me listen to Elgar."

I went out to the kitchen. Everything was ready. I uncorked a bottle of Gewürztraminer and got Tina, while Bea ferried the food to the dining room table. The conversation was mostly a monologue by Tina attempting to answer the question why Elgar gave up composing music for recording music. No definite conclusion was reached.

We were in the living room, pie eaten, tea drunk, and halfway into the movie *Never Let Me Go*, when the doorbell rang. I went to the door, turned on the light, saw it was Gwen, and invited her in.

"We're in the living room, come on. Although we'll probably move to the office."

"Is Tina healing okay, Harry?"

"I think so."

"Glad to hear it."

Gwen and I walked into the living room. She went to Tina, gave her a hug and bussed her cheek, did the same to Bea, and sat down. I felt left out. To my surprise, Tina didn't make us relocate to the office.

"What do you have for me, Gwen? Harry, get Gwen pie and…"

"Hot water is okay, Harry. Is the pastry your oil pastry?"

"It is."

"Apple pie?"

"Right on."

She gave me a thumbs up and I got her pie and hot water. She took a bite of pie and I was pleased to see the look of satisfaction take over her face. She chewed and swallowed and began her report.

"I got a lot of stuff off their phones, Tina. What I found most interesting were the text messages to Opal Snyder on Brewer's phone. Opal's the receptionist and also appears to be Brewer's spy."

Tina smiled. "The plot thickens."

"It does. Opal is apparently one of Alex's nieces."

"Well, I'll be doggone," I said. "Brewer has everyone against her, so she brings in family to turn the tables on them."

Gwen took a bite of pie before continuing. "Right, Harry. From what I can gather, Opal listened in on the calls made from the office phones. She was able to gather lots of information that way."

"Well that explains why she's always there," I said.

Tina pursed her lips, rested her chin on tented fingers, and closed her eyes. She stayed that way for a good five minutes before opening eyes and issuing orders. "We need to talk to Opal. Harry, have Cal bring her here. I doubt she'll come on her own. I also want you to find out everything you can on her. Gwen, talk to her neighbors. Harry, call David and Ed and have them tail her, starting as soon as possible. I want to know Opal's Achilles Heel. The frontal assault didn't work with Brewer. The strong man, however, is strongest alone. So let's see if her partner in crime wilts when a little heat is applied."

33

THE FAT LADY GETS READY TO SING

Sunday. October 12th

MY BIRTHDAY. NUMBER FIFTY-FIVE. UNFORTUNATELY, WE WERE SMACK dab in the middle of a case.

At breakfast, my ladies wished me a happy birthday and Tina really made my day by informing me we'd be going to the Gasthof for lunch. Now that was a treat. I'm an unabashed Anglophile, but German food ranks a close second and Gasthof zur Gemutlichkeit serves the best German food in the Cities, in my opinion.

In addition, not wanting to wait, my ladies gave me my birthday gifts at breakfast, not that I minded one bit. I got a beautiful camel hair cardigan from Bea and a case of Warre's Warrior Porto from Tina.

Gwen had gotten her marching orders last night direct from the Boss. I texted David and Ed and gave them instructions. They texted back to let me know they were available and would be tailing Opal as soon as possible. I called Cal right after breakfast and he said he'd bring her over, probably some time this afternoon.

After breakfast, we received a text from David letting us know Opal was at work. I passed the information on to Cal.

The remainder of the morning I looked up what I could on Brewer's niece, courtesy of the internet. Just before noon, when we were getting ready to head out to the restaurant, Gwen called in to report the people in Opal's apartment building had little information for us. She was a nice person, quiet, and stayed to herself. Most importantly, Gwen found out the apartment above Opal's was vacant.

Tina was all smiles and took the phone from me. "Gwen, ask the landlord or manager if you can rent the apartment by the day. If not, rent it for the month. If he or she balks, say it's police business and give them Cal's name and number. Install listening devices and monitor her." After a brief pause, Tina said "goodbye" and handed the phone back to me.

Business taken care of, we drove over to the Gasthof in Northeast Minneapolis and had a fabulous meal. Tina had something with sauerkraut, Bea had a sausage and noodle dish, and I had Hasenpfeffer. Bea drank beer, Tina and I had wine. By two we were back home. Good thing, too, for Cal was in his car parked out front of our place with Opal Snyder sitting in the back seat.

Car parked, we went into the house by the back door. Tina and I went to our desks and Bea got the front door. Where I am sure Cal was waiting because Tina and I hadn't even started on getting our chairs warm when Bea ushered in our guests. Opal was clearly pissed.

"Okay, Miss Wright, I'm here. What do you want? We're going to sue for harassment. You know that, don't you?"

"Ms. Snyder, please have a seat," Tina said.

Opal sat where Tina had indicated. The oxblood oversized wingback. She looked tiny in the chair.

My sister continued. "I don't scare, Ms. Snyder. What I've endured in the line of duty makes *Nightmare on Elm Street* look like a Disney cartoon. Sue me if you so desire. When I'm done with you, you might get out of prison in twenty years with good behavior."

"Prison? What are you talking about?"

"I'm talking about accessory to murder, Ms. Snyder."

"What *are* you talking about? I haven't killed anyone and I don't know anyone who has."

"Your job at the campaign is not only receptionist, but also to spy on the other staffers by listening in on their telephone conversations. That is correct. Isn't it?"

"I don't know what you're talking about."

"You're Alex Brewer's niece. Are you not?"

Opal wasn't too good at hiding her surprise. She did, though, make a valiant effort. "So what if I am?"

"Were you her spy?"

"I did my job and if I wasn't here I'd be doing my job right now."

"That doesn't answer my question, Ms. Snyder. Did you spy on your colleagues as part of your job and pass the information on to your aunt, Alex Brewer?"

Opal hesitated too long before answering. "No."

"Then what about the text message sent to you three days before Damon Rossiter died? Your aunt texted, and I quote, 'Good job, Opal. This is exactly what I need.' My question to you, Ms. Snyder, is what information did you obtain? What 'good job' did you do?"

"How did you get that? You're spying."

"Of course. It's my job. First I was a snoop for the US government and now I'm a snoop for private citizens and occasionally the police. My job is to spy on people. And now I'm spying on you, just like you spied on your co-workers. Only I will find out every dirty little secret in your life. Nothing will be private. I'll know every time you flush the toilet, open your refrigerator, and fuck somebody."

"You can't. That's not legal."

"Of course, it's legal. I just can't harass you and unless certain precautions are taken it can't be admitted in a court of law as evidence. Don't you listen to the news? Haven't you heard about Snowden? The government spies on us all the time. From the Feds right on down to the local police force. There is no privacy in America anymore. And there will be none for you either. I will ruin your life. Everyone is interested in information and I will sell it for top dollar. Kiss your insurance company goodbye. Your bank. Your credit rating. Your credit card. Your friends."

"You are an evil person."

"No, I'm not. I'm exposing a person who either committed murder or aided and abetted the commission of murder. You see, Opal, I had a license to kill given to me by the US government. Unfortunately, you don't. Yet, because of your actions, four people are dead and a fifth maimed for life. You are the one, Opal Snyder, who may be sued by Prisca Thoraldson and maybe even Madelyn Horstman."

Opal was beaten. You could see it in the look on her face. I got the box of tissues ready.

"What did Aunt Alex promise you for you to keep quiet?"

"I didn't know! Honest! She promised me an important job in Washington and a car and a house if, if I helped her. I didn't know she was going to kill anyone. Honest."

Tina had thrown a sucker pitch and Opal had swung at it. My sister looked at Cal and doggone it if she didn't have a smile on her face. "I think she's all yours."

He nodded and walked up to Opal. After reading her rights to her, he said, "Let's go down to the station and you can tell me everything you know."

Opal nodded, stood up, and walked out with Cal, but not before the final indignity of him putting handcuffs on her.

I looked over at my sister. Her chin was resting on steepled fingers.

The strong man is strongest alone. Brewer was a tough nut to crack. Her niece was just a scared little kid. A product of a sheltered suburban life and totally ignorant of what real life is all about. The fat lady was stepping out onto the stage and getting ready to sing. Her aria was going to be a sweet song. A very sweet song.

34

FINALE

Thursday. October 16th

SUNDAY, AFTER OPAL AND CAL LEFT OUR PLACE, TINA CALLED Harold Feingold, apprised him of the situation and suggested that Opal Snyder might appreciate his services. Yesterday morning, in appreciation of the tip, a dozen yellow roses were delivered and are in a vase on Tina's desk. The card he sent with the flowers was filled with an effusive declaration of thanks.

Cal got a complete confession out of Opal in exchange for an immunity deal worked out on her behalf by Feingold. Tuesday afternoon, Feingold called to let us know Brewer had been arrested that morning. With receipt of the news, I phoned David, Gwen, and Ed, told them the party was over, and to step around at their earliest convenience with their reports and hours so I could give each of them their pay.

This afternoon Cal stopped by and Tina agreed to see him, since it was business.

He took his usual seat in the oxblood oversized wingback, which isn't oversized for him. "I just wanted to give you an update on the case."

Her voice wasn't icy when she said, "Go ahead", but it wasn't warm like a summer day either.

Cal ignored it and went on. "In a plea bargain, Brewer confessed to all four murders."

"Did you find the gun?" Tina asked.

"We did. It was in a storage unit off Hiawatha listed in her niece's name. Opal didn't know anything about it. So she claimed and I'm inclined to believe her. Brewer's sentencing is in a couple months. She's looking at four life sentences. Possibility of parole after thirty years."

"That's a sweet deal for her. Palmquist must know somebody."

"Probably. It's all politics. You know that."

"I do. Any word on Horstman's reaction?"

"Couldn't believe it, of course. The woman's in denial. What's there not to believe?"

"She going on with her campaign?"

"I don't think she's officially withdrawing. She'll probably go through the motions, but I don't think her heart is in it."

"Maybe she can take over her husband's company. Do something productive with her life."

Cal smiled. "Maybe. Well, I don't have anything more for you. I would like to say this was good. Working with you. Kind of like old times. Hope we can do it again."

"Don't get those hopes or anything else up, Swenson. I haven't forgiven you."

"I didn't say you did. I was just saying we work well together and I hope we can work together again sometime."

"And I'm saying—"

"I know what you're saying, Wright. I do understand English, you know. Have yourself a good day." He stood and started for the door to leave and then turned back. "How's your leg?"

"It's healing. Thanks for asking."

"Glad to hear it and don't mention it." He gave me a nod and left.

"Well, Sis, it looks like another case has come to a successful conclusion. What I want to know, though, is what if Opal hadn't cracked. Then what?"

She poured herself a glass of madeira and lit a cigar. After a cloud of smoke was on its way to the ceiling, she said, "There were other weak links in the chain and it would have been simply a matter of finding their Achilles's Heel. We lucked out in finding the weakest link first."

"On a different note, what about Cal?"

Her pleasant demeanor evaporated. "What about him?"

"It seemed to me, you two—"

"Forget it, Harry."

"Come on, Tina. You can't tell me you don't have feelings for the guy."

"Why can't you and Bea drop it? Cal and I are done."

"How can you say that? You two are meant for each other. Are you going to let one bad episode override all the good ones?"

"This conversation is over. Don't bring it up again. Do you understand me?"

I stood and walked to the door. Before leaving, I turned around and looked at her. "You are a fool, Tina. You can fix your own supper. Bea and I are eating out." I opened the door, walked out, and closed it behind me.

Bea and I did go out to eat and when we came back I found a note informing us the head honcho was in her room and was not to be disturbed.

I dished up ice cream for my honey and me and we sat in the living room. Going through the selections, we decided to watch an episode of *Midsomer Murders* on Netflix. We like the show, even though Bea isn't keen on murder mysteries as a general rule. When the episode was over, we headed upstairs to bed.

On the way, she said, "Life is too short. Any moment we can die. I have to get them back together. Tina helped us get together. It's the least I can do."

35

EPILOGUE

Thursday. November 6th

ABSENCE MAKES THE HEART GROW FONDER. SO THEY SAY. WHOEVER *they* are. In the preceding three weeks, with plenty of money in the bank, Tina turned down four potential clients and an offer to consult with the Minneapolis police department on a homicide case, which prompted Cal to once again try to mend the fences, only to get stiff-armed once again by Tina.

Also in the preceding three weeks Madelyn Horstman lost in a landslide, Vi Nguyen stopped by to apologize for treating us so poorly, we heard Prisca Thoraldson filed a civil suit against Alex Brewer and Opal Snyder and is asking for ten million dollars in compensation due to her permanent nerve damage, and Bea launched her "we want Cal" campaign.

Twice Tina came very close to terminating our jobs. We were saved by my appeal to family and Bea's apologies.

Today, however, like Lee's assault on Cemetery Ridge in the Battle of Gettysburg, Bea was making one last attempt to break through Tina's resistance.

Cal was sitting in the waiting room. Contrary to Tina's orders,

Bea had let him in. She could do so, because Tina had gone out to the art store to get a couple tubes of paint. I'd advised Bea against it, but if I've learned one thing in life it is that you can't tell anyone what to do. Especially family and your spouse. So I said nothing and if Tina ripped Bea a new one or threw us out, well, what could I say? Tina had already warned her. But just as Tina had helped Bea and I get together, so Bea was going to return the favor. Or at least try to.

Tina came in through the back door and therefore wasn't immediately aware of Cal's presence. He having wisely parked down the street.

When Bea saw her, she simply said, "Tina, there's someone to see you in the waiting room."

"Who?" she asked.

"Someone who needs to see you. Come on."

Tina followed Bea and I followed Tina. When Tina saw Cal, she turned around to leave and I said, "You need to talk. If for nothing else so you both have closure."

"You two have conspired against me. I'll never forgive you."

I said, "Never say 'never'. Hear him out and then decide."

She was pissed, royally pissed, and I could tell Bea was of the same opinion as I — maybe we had made a mistake. However, we'd crossed the Rubicon and there was no going back. Tina stood before Cal, looked down at him, and said, "Speak."

He stood. "Tina, I'm sorry. What I did was bad. Very bad. We've known each other for a long time and there was no reason I should have treated you like I did. We've been friends and lovers and I think we love each other. If you no longer love me, I understand. But I, well, I love you and I thought about you even when... Well, I never stopped thinking about you and when Nikki and I split up, I knew I'd probably ruined the best thing that'd ever happened to me and that is you.

"If you can't forgive me, I understand. But I'm asking you to please give me one more chance. I'm not too proud to beg for your forgiveness. We're good together, you and I, and you were right: we are a team. You are my partner. You are my real partner. I love you, Tina." He took a ring out of his pocket. "This is probably not the time to say this, but I may not get another chance so here goes. Tina Wright, I love you and want you to be my partner forever. Will you marry me?"

FROM ME TO YOU

I hope you enjoyed *The Conspiracy Game*. If you did, please leave a review where you bought the book and on your favorite social media sites. Your review is like word of mouth advertising. And it is pure gold.

Become one of my VIP Readers! You'll get a free copy of *Vampire House and Other Early Cases of Justinia Wright, P.I.* and join the exciting and delicious world of Justinia Wright! You'll get curated and exclusive content, news, and other good stuff.

Sign up today for your free book at BookFunnel! Just click, tap, or scan the QR code!

From Me to You

CONTINUE THE ADVENTURE!

If you enjoyed *The Conspiracy Game*, Tina and Harry's adventures continue in *A Nest of Spies*.

Tina's past comes back to haunt her when a former coworker from The Company wants her help to obtain stolen plans for a secret weapon. When other associates from her past want to hire her to find those same plans, Tina begins to see dollar signs.

But things are never simple. When the FBI gets involved and wants to invoke the Patriot Act, and when bodies start to fall, will Tina be able to deliver the goods and make a big payday? Or will she disappear, courtesy of the Patriot Act?

Click, tap, or scan the QR code to get your copy today!

ALSO BY CW HAWES

I'm a multi-genre author, because more genres means more fun!

I currently have books in the mystery, horror/weird/paranormal, post-apocalyptic, and alternative history/dieselpunk genres.

Please take a look at the My Books page on my website to see all the worlds I inhabit and write about.

Just click, scan, or tap the QR code!

ABOUT CW HAWES

CW Hawes is a playwright, award winning poet, and fictioneer. He is also the author of the bestselling *Death Wears a Crimson Hat*.

His interests are wide ranging and this is reflected in both the genres and the contents of his books.

You can visit him at his website. Just click, tap, or scan the QR code.